HEROIC LADS AND LASSES EVERYWHERE HAVE ALSO READ THESE OTHER THRILLING TALES OF PALS IN PERIL

Whales on Stilts!

The Clue of the Linoleum Lederhosen

Jasper Dash and the Flame-Pits of Delaware

Agent Q, or The Smell of Danger!

Zombie Mommy

A Pals in Peril Tale

HE LAUGHED WITH HIS OTHER MOUTHS

M. T. ANDERSON
Illustrations by **KURT CYRUS**

BEACH LANE BOOKS

NEW YORK   LONDON

TORONTO   SYDNEY   NEW DELHI

In memory of my Great-Uncle Charles

BEACH LANE BOOKS
An imprint of Simon & Schuster Children's Publishing Division
1230 Avenue of the Americas, New York, New York 10020

Text copyright © 2014 by M. T. Anderson
Interior illustrations copyright © 2014 by Kurt Cyrus
Jacket illustration copyright © 2014 by Brandon Dorman

BEACH LANE BOOKS is a trademark of Simon & Schuster, Inc.
For information about special discounts for bulk purchases, please contact
Simon & Schuster Special Sales at 1-866-506-1949
or business@simonandschuster.com.
The Simon & Schuster Speakers Bureau can bring authors to your live event.
For more information or to book an event, contact the Simon & Schuster Speakers
Bureau at 1-866-248-3049 or visit our website at www.simonspeakers.com.
Book design by Debra Sfetsios-Conover
The text for this book is set in Stempel Garamond.
Manufactured in the United States of America
0714 FFG
First Edition
2 4 6 8 10 9 7 5 3 1
Library of Congress Cataloging-in-Publication Data
Anderson, M. T.
He laughed with his other mouths / M.T. Anderson ; illustrations by Kurt Cyrus. —
First edition.
pages cm — (A pals in peril tale ; [6])
Summary: "In this sixth Pals in Peril adventure, Jasper Dash is off into the universe
to search for his long lost father!"— Provided by publisher.
ISBN 978-1-4424-5110-0 (hardcover) — ISBN 978-1-4424-5115-5 (ebook)
[1. Adventure and adventurers—Fiction. 2. Extraterrestrial beings—Fiction.
3. Humorous stories.] I. Cyrus, Kurt, illustrations. II. Title.
PZ7.A54395He 2014
[Fic]—dc23
2013034710

HE LAUGHED
WITH HIS OTHER MOUTHS

PROLOGUE:
INCIDENT ON OPPOSITE DAY

The moon was not the only thing glowing in the sky that January night. Other things soared over the white farms and forests. Things watched the cold Earth carefully. Things peered down at the hills and the little houses and the fir trees on the mountainsides.

From a mile above, a car looks like a very tiny thing. Just like a toy.

Inside the car, there was a lot of noise. The Delb family drove home from their skiing vacation. Mom Delb drove. Dad Delb slept. And their two kids, Grady and Hopper, fought in the backseat, slapping each other's heads.

"You're stupid."

"You're junk."

"You're broken, and don't touch my pillow."

"Touch. Touch. Touch."

"I said you're broken, and don't touch my pillow!"

"Touch. Touch. Touch."

"Mom!"

"Which one of you is that?"

"Hopper. I told Grady not to touch my pillow."

Mom said, "Don't touch his pillow, Grady."

"Mom? What day is it?"

"Umm, the sixth of January."

"Oh, wow, I think it's Opposite Day! So that means I got to do the opposite of whatever people say! Touch touch touch. Touch touch touch."

"Hey! Stop touching my pillow! You're stupid!"

"Opposite Day! You mean I'm smart!"

"You're a pig-hog!"

"Opposite Day! You mean I'm an angel made from gold."

They had been arguing this way for hours. They did not pay attention to anything outside the car.

On either side of the road, everything was white and silent. There were steep white pastures. The windows of small white houses were dark. The white smoke from woodstoves and furnaces rose quietly into a black sky frosted with stars. There were forests of spruce with their dangling arms all sleeved and gloved in snow.

Then, above the trees, there was motion. To see it, Grady Delb and Hopper Delb would have had to look backward. They didn't. They were too busy punching each other.

Hopper had figured out the trick of Opposite

Day. Now he was saying, "You're handsome, Grady! You're the most handsome anywhere!"

"Thank you. I know I am."

"No, you said it was Opposite Day!"

"It just was over. Clang! Opposite Day over! I'm handsome! You said it! It sticks! I'm glue!"

"Actually, Grady?" said Mrs. Delb. "It's not midnight yet. About three minutes. So it must still be Opposite Day."

"Ha!" said Hopper, and he began to throw every compliment he could at his brother. "Hey, Grady, you're smart! You're a real brain casserole. No: Opposite Day! You're a great person. Opposite Day! Every girl on the slopes from every town thought you were cool. Opposite Day!"

"Make him stop!" said Grady. "Make him stop saying opposites!"

Then a shadow fell across them. Something had blocked out the moon.

Hopper said, "You're going to have a long and successful life. Oppos—"

Hopper noticed Grady gaping at something

behind them. They both looked out the back window.

The trees on either side went like an aisle. Above them, sliding along through the stars, was a glowing shape. Its lights were bright.

Something was following them.

The Delb children looked around wildly.

The car was passing through a deep, dark forest. There was no one around them except whoever hung above them.

"Mom . . . ," hissed Grady. "Mom. There's a ship."

"Hmm?" said Mom Delb.

"A flying saucer," whispered Grady. "Right behind us."

"What? Hopper, what's Grady saying?"

The saucer swung down lower. It played beams over the fleeing car.

Hopper didn't know what to do. He wanted to warn his parents too, but he wasn't very smart, and he really believed it was Opposite Day. "Mom!" he squealed in terror. "Grady is

5

absolutely wrong! There isn't a flying saucer at all!"

Grady screamed, "We're being chased by aliens!" and Hopper hollered his agreement: "No! We aren't! We really aren't, Mom! Go slower—*now!* Slower, Mom!"

"What are you two talking about?"

"A flying saucer!"

"No flying saucer!"

Mom Delb chuckled. "Could you make a decision and then get back to me?"

Hopper insisted desperately, "Mom, there is *no hovering spaceship with red lights lowering itself right over the car, chasing us, blocking out the sky like some rogue evil moon, come down to Earth to wreak havoc among all mankind! OPPOSITE DAY!*"

"Hey," said Dad Delb, waking up. "What's all the noise?"

"There is a— } SPACESHIP CHASING
"There is no— } US!" the two kids yelled.

"You see what I put up with?" said Mom Delb. She said, "Okay. You first. Hopper, what is it you want to say?"

"SLOWER, MOM! DRIVE SLOWER! THERE IS NO, ABSOLUTELY NO, GLOWING FLYING SAUCER WITH—"

"Oops! Midnight," sang Mom Delb. "If it was Opposite Day, it's over now!"

But it was too late. Light flooded the car.

Then all lights went off.

The engine stalled. The car coasted a few feet, the wheels crackling on frost.

It came to rest.

The family all heard each other's breath tremble. All Delbs were terrified.

There was no glow from above. Everything was gray. Metal was gray, and the frozen road, and the distant fields of snow.

Dad Delb pressed a button to roll down his window. It clicked, but nothing rolled.

Carefully, they all opened their doors. They stepped out of their car. They raised their eyes above the prongs of their skis, which were clipped to the roof.

Four curls of breath steamed in the air.

Above them was a huge, dark thing. It hung there, blocking out the sky.

A breeze moved through the forest, and the tops of the fir trees swayed. The object above them didn't move at all.

For a while, they stared up at it. It didn't seem like it made sense to try to run away.

And then the lights of the ship came on.

The family stumbled.

The snow had hardened in the cold, and there was a hard crust on it. The reflection of red lights shot along the furrows and the sloped fields.

The ruddy glow lit even the dark, squashed places deep in the forest: the weird, tangled limbs, the pimpled bark.

* * *

In the morning, all four Delbs woke up. There was a rushing noise. Bright white light. They shot up in their seats. They were belted down. Dad Delb yelped.

Phew! They were just in their car. They were by the side of a major highway. Traffic was shooting past. Grady had just been asleep and drooling on Hopper's pillow.

They all looked around. They were confused. They had some dim memory. . . . Hadn't they seen something? Above them? And hadn't they been taken to a white, glowing place? Where someone had questioned them, asking them again and again a question that they had not understood:

Where is Jasper Dash? The human called Jasper Dash? Where is he?

They did not know. They had no idea who Jasper Dash was. Even now, they had trouble remembering their dream. It faded. They did not talk about it.

Mom Delb started up the family car.

Without speaking, they drove toward coffee.

SCIENCE UNFAIR

"Jasper Dash!" a voice called. "Someone is looking for you!"

Jasper Dash, Boy Technonaut, looked up from his welding torch. He was putting the final touches on his science fair project. He shut off the torch's bright white flame. He lifted the visor of his welding helmet to see who was speaking to him.

It was a teacher. They were in the school cafeteria. Everyone was setting up their science fair projects on folding tables. Kids had drawn posters on foam core. They had ant farms and pet iguanas. They had videos to show. Jasper Dash had a fifteen-foot-tall, mysterious machine with a built-in nuclear reactor.

You have probably never heard of Jasper

Dash, Boy Technonaut. Once, he was famous. He invented rocket cars and submarines and even a bicycle that drilled to the center of the Earth. He was, in fact, the hero of a series of old books with names like *Jasper Dash and His Amazing Interplanetary Runabout, Jasper Dash and His Incredible Undersea Drill, Jasper Dash and His Attractive Photon Sweater, Jasper Dash on Death Mesa,* and *Jasper Dash: Beyond Space! And Under Time!**

---

* Not available in stores near you. Not available at your favorite online retailer. Available only at church rummage sales, usually stuffed in boxes under an old brass chandelier and some knitwear, next to the bag of mildewed finger puppets. You move aside the dusty chandelier, and there's this book from the 1930s or 1940s, and on the cover is a blond-haired boy full of pluck and adventure. He's running away from some gunmen side by side with a robot. The robot looks dumb and old-fashioned. It is built entirely from metal boxes, with a stupid-looking face on it. In fact, the robot looks so dumb that you feel bad for it. You know that it doesn't know how dumb it looks. It kind of breaks your heart. You don't want anyone else to laugh at the robot. So you actually pick up the book and you pay the church ladies ten cents for it, and then you look and see that there are more books from the series, and you pay ten cents for them, too. You are on vacation, and you figure that it somehow feels right to be reading oldy-timey books in the little house your family is renting by the lake, where the loons call at night and motorboats skip along the flat water by day.

When you get back to your family's car, you have a rumpled paper grocery bag full of Jasper Dash books. They smell like mold. Everyone looks at you like you were crazy to buy them. Crinkling up the top of the bag, you realize you are probably never going to bother to read them, not in a thousand years.

He was a blond-haired boy full of pluck and adventure. He fought evil and greed with both fists, which left his feet free to scissor-kick wicked German barons.

Unfortunately, no one really reads Jasper's books anymore. He has not aged or changed since his books originally came out, back in the twentieth century. He has always been thirteen or so, and is always inventing rockets and radio-control airplanes. Back in the day, millions of kids had read his adventures. Hundreds of thousands had crammed their closets with his cardboard zap guns and die-cast metal spaceships and decoder scarves. Now, no one read his books other than his friends.

Luckily, Jasper didn't care about fame and fortune. He didn't care about much other than his inventions—and truth and justice, of course.

"Thank you, Ms. Shellberg," he said. "Who is it who's looking for me?"

"One of the students . . . Lily Gefelty. She

said she's helping you with your presentation. I saw her looking for you over there. Should I tell her where your booth is?"

"Yes, please, ma'am!" said Jasper. "Lily's going to pull the sheet off my invention!"

The teacher smiled at him and secretly hoped this time the invention wouldn't have mechanical tentacles. She went off to find Lily.

Jasper didn't go to school, and hadn't for a long time, but he was always invited to participate in the school's science fair. Recently, however, the principal and the school board had talked about leaving him out. He always meant well, of course, but somehow Jasper's inventions did not seem to work as well as they had back in the last century, in the 1930s, forties, and fifties. In the last few years, in fact, his science fair inventions had occasionally malfunctioned and caused problems, and one of them had even ended up roaring,

"TREMBLE BEFORE ME!"

which no one, least of all Jasper, appreciated.

His new, big machine lurked under its white sheet.

Lily Gefelty ran to his side. "Hey, Jas!" she said. "Are you ready?"

Jasper knelt, tinkering with some bolts. "Absolutely," he said. He rapped softly on the metal. "Why, this gizmo is going to knock your socks off."

Lily grinned. She loved his enthusiasm. "What is it?" she asked. "What does it do?"

Before he could answer, there was a loud, crowing laugh from the next booth. It was a group of the school's jerks. They were pointing at Jasper's project and cackling.

One of them asked, "What is it this year, boy wonder?"

They said, "You always have the stupidest machines."

Jasper did not look at them. He just fell silent and pretended to shine his contraption's hubcaps.

"Don't pay any attention," whispered Lily.

One of the jerks yelled, "The only reason

anyone ever comes to the science fair is to see what stupid thing you'll do next."

"I believe," said Jasper, with dignity, "that you will all be surprised and dumbfounded when you see what I have come up with this year." He inspected their project, then tried to be friendly by saying, "And may I say that I hope your chemical analysis of orange spray-cheese is warmly received by an inquisitive public."

The jerks laughed again and turned away. They leaned against their table.

"Don't think about them," said Lily. "Everyone thinks you're great."

Jasper said, "My last few science fair projects have perhaps not been very successful. Though what is success? I do not think many youngsters have ever transported a whole kindergarten class to another dimension. And gotten them back. All of them."* He cleared his throat. "Plus an extra student who we never

* In Jasper Dash #63: *Jasper Dash and the Hyperspace Naptime.*

could explain. Isn't that a kind of victory? I try so hard. . . ."

"You're going to be super today," said Lily. "No matter what your invention is."

"Super *stupid*," added one of the jerks from the next booth over.

Lily flinched and didn't know what to say.

She was a very shy person. Her hair hung in front of her eyes, and she liked the fact that it hid her face a little. When she needed to see something interesting, she blew her bangs out of her eyes. She wished sometimes that she could just watch the world while floating around invisibly, and never be seen or heard.

Now that they were being made fun of, she felt particularly shy. She was silent. She and Jasper didn't look at each other. The Boy Technonaut stood up, put down his wrench, and wiped his hands on his shorts.

"Okeydokey," he said. "Whenever that crowd comes in, we'll be ready for them."

When all the exhibits in the Pelt Science Fair

were ready, the teachers would throw open the doors to the dining hall, and all the parents and kids waiting outside would come in. There would be a little speech by the principal, Mr. Krome, and then they'd invite their special guest, Jasper Dash, Boy Technonaut, to unveil his newest creation. Then refreshments would be served and everyone could spend a pleasant hour at the different tables finding out about the life cycle of locusts and the different strata of the Earth's crust.

Jasper and Lily stood anxiously and whispered to each other about the way she was going to pull the sheet off the invention. Lily had practiced at home, on the dining room table. She had discovered a special flick of the wrists so that the cloth would whoosh up and then float gently down. She wanted everything to go perfectly for Jasper.

It was time. The teachers opened the doors. Everyone filed in, shaking hands and gossiping. Parents who hadn't seen one another for

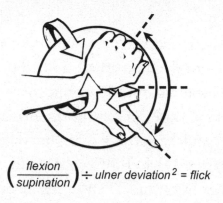

$$\left(\frac{\textit{flexion}}{\textit{supination}}\right) \div \textit{ulner deviation}^2 = \textit{flick}$$

months waved across the room. Kids were squirming, excited to show off their butterflies and seismometers.

Mr. Krome, the principal, tall and business-like, bustled up to Jasper. "We're almost ready," Mr. Krome said. "Please, please don't blow us all up."

"Have I ever blown you up, Mr. Krome?"

"No. The fuse was damp." The principal looked around. "Do you have a parent any-where? Is your father coming or something?"

This was not a very sensitive question to ask. Jasper blinked and looked down at the floor. Then he said awkwardly, "I, um, never knew my father."

"Oh. I'm so sorry," said Mr. Krome, embarrassed. "I just want someone here in case another one of your projects starts yelling, 'Kneel and obey.' And calls the teachers 'puny human rubbish.'"

"Yes, I . . . why, there's my mother. Over there. Say, hi there, Mom!"

Jasper's mother, Dolores Dash, swept over, taking Jasper's hands in her own. She had once been an astronomer. Jasper Dash did not really have a father. He had been created by a highly concentrated beam of information projected from the region of the Horsehead Nebula.

Mrs. Dash was dressed in a sharp, sherbet-green suit. Her hair was swirled and piled up in a big, classy bell on her head. "Jasper, honey," she said. "I'm so excited! Why, hello, Mr. Krome. You are so kind to ask Jasper to partici-pate in the science fair again. You should know that Jasper has been working on his project for weeks. It's a big secret. He won't say a single peep about it to anyone."

Jasper smiled shyly.

"Great," said Mr. Krome. "And now you're going to spring it on an unsuspecting world."

"I certainly am," said Jasper.

The principal sighed. "You ready?"

"Mr. Krome," said Jasper, "I spread 'ready' on my sandwiches."

"I know you do," said Mr. Krome. "Just remember, 'Accidental Death' is a lunch counter I don't want to visit."

Jasper nodded. "There will be no problems. Cross my heart," he said, "and hope to . . . um . . ."

The principal raised his eyebrow.

"Never mind," said Jasper.

It was time. Mr. Krome swiveled and clapped his hands. He held up an arm. He clapped his hands again. Finally the crowd quieted down.

"Hello, parents and children of Pelt! It's a fun day! A day I'm sure you always look forward to! Your kids have been working hard on their projects for weeks. I can't wait to walk around and see what they've cooked up for us.

"It's so important that we foster scientific creativity in our schools, if we want this great nation to stay on the cutting edge of innovation and technology. That's why we've invited Jasper Dash, Boy Technonaut, to show us one of his new inventions. Jasper has been creating inventions since the 1930s! And he doesn't look a day over thirteen!" (Uneasy laugh from the crowd. In fact, Jasper was thirteen. Or about a hundred, depending on how you counted.) "Take it away, Jasper!"

Everyone applauded. They strained forward to see. Some of the boys hoped the experiment would be a big disaster and something sloppy and dangerous and alien would stumble out of it.

Jasper stood next to the invention. Behind him, Lily was ready to pull the sheet off.

"People of Pelt," said Jasper. "What I am going to show you may amaze you. But I swear to you—someday, *every one of you* will own one of these devices. Time and progress move swiftly! You have to jog like billy-o or you'll be left behind. But, fellows, you can always get an update on which way progress is heading with *THIS dandy contraption*!"

At that, Lily, pale with anxiety, whipped the sheet off the machine.

Everyone gasped. They couldn't tell what it was. It was complicated and as big as a lunch cart and had an antenna on top. It had huge metal wheels. It had a little door on the side with an atom painted on it. It had some kind of dial and a headset on it.

The crowd gaped. You could have heard a pin drop.

Jasper smiled. "So. We just flick on the nuclear reactor here . . . and . . . voilà!"

The machine started to chug. Jasper Dash picked up the headset and fitted it on over his mouth and one ear. With a great deal of drama, he extended one finger. He reached toward the dial.

He cranked the dial around, and it sprang back in a circle, rattling. He did this several times. Then he waited.

The whole crowd waited: girls with sarcastic expressions, mothers with strollers, grandmothers in pleated jeans, a few soccer jocks who hated dorks like Jasper Dash, antsy brainiacs, and Lily, who couldn't wait to see what would happen next. All of them stared.

And the phone on the lunchroom wall rang.

Mr. Krome looked over at it, annoyed.

It rang again. And again.

"Pick it up!" said Jasper, delighted.

Mr. Krome walked over and got the phone.

Jasper said, "Mr. Krome? It's me! Calling . . . from the first—the very first—*fully mobile telephone!*" He waved at the principal across the room. "See? See this? You just drag this cart with you, and occasionally put in some uranium ingots, and you can make calls—*to anywhere within this town!*" He was practically crowing with pride.

People were perplexed. Then they were surprised. Had he really invented a mobile phone the size of a truck?

People coughed. They exchanged winks

with one another. The school jerks started snickering. Then other people laughed quietly.

Lily's heart sank. She saw the crowd chuckling. She saw kids pointing at Jasper and whispering.

Jasper was not always aware of what was going on in the world around him. He came from a different, older America, and did not understand the modern world very well—which is surprising, considering that he thought only of the future.

But he understood he had done something wrong.

"You don't understand," he said. Now he could almost not be heard over the laughter. He was blushing. "You don't understand! This phone has its own engine! It's not hard to pull! It will drive right beside you!" He took a few steps and the contraption chugged along beside him, clanking like roadwork.

Kids only laughed harder.

"No! Wait!" he said.

Lily couldn't stand that he kept going. She wanted to tell him to stop. He was no longer blushing. He was as pale as a ghost, because there was no blood left in his face.

Jasper insisted, "Look! We'll call the mayor! With our *fully mobile telephone*! I have the number right here!"

"Shut up!" yelled one of the school jerks. "Take a seat, flyboy!"

"Lily!" called Jasper desperately. "I'm going to make the call! Start shoveling atomic fuel!" He dialed the phone.

Lily loyally opened the little door with the atom on it. She took a shovel and scooped pellets from the uranium scuttle into the hopper.

She could hear people say, "Who *is* he, anyway?" "This is stupid." "He's in some kind of old-timey books. They're really dumb and boring."

Lily glared out at the crowd as she fed the nuclear reactor. She glanced at Jasper's face. She could tell he'd heard every word. He had turned away from the crowd. He was almost crying. He still had on the headset.

"Mr. Mayor?" she heard him say, hopefully. "Are you there? . . . You are? . . . Yes, I'm at the Pelt Science Fair, and I wonder whether you'd tell the great people of Pelt that—"

"I know where you are," said the mayor, standing right behind Jasper. "I'm here to see my daughter explain how a rainbow works. You called my cell."

Jasper turned, astonished. He saw the glowing thing in the mayor's hand.

At that, he staggered backward.

"Oh my," he said. "Oh my. All of you . . . already have . . . ?"

Lily stopped shoveling. She bit her lip and hid behind her bangs.

The mayor nodded. He patted Jasper on the shoulder. He walked away.

The school jerks walked over from their cheese molecule and began kicking the machine's wheels. They began pushing it back and forth and screeching around corners. Jasper didn't even notice. He didn't even move.

Lily stood next to him.

"This is the last straw," he said. "I wish I could just disappear."

He did not know, but he would soon get his wish.

"I guess," he said sadly, "that maybe instead, I should have showed them my matter transporter that can take a man instantaneously to the stars."

St Norman's Episcopal Church
Annual Summer
RUMMAGE SALE!!!

YOUR SOURCE FOR: Old Nightstands! Side Tables! Unmatched Silverware! Half a Girl's Bike! Barbies Missing One High-Heel Shoe! O'Dermott's Restaurant Kidz Meal Novelty Drinking Glasses (featuring Frank the Fry-O-Later Gator)! And plenty of books from the old Jasper Dash, Boy Technonaut Series, including: *Jasper Dash on Explosion Island! Jasper Dash on the Trail of the Star Chompers! Jasper Dash and His Remarkable Electron Rattle! Jasper Dash and the Lost Bayou Friend Boat Mystery—Under the Sea!* Guarantee: These books have not been read by anybody for a *long, long, long* time! Or touched!

Also available: Several volumes in the Horror Hollow Series, starring Katie Mulligan, including *A Week at Camp Rot-Grub, Morning of the Mutants,* and *Monster Spit III: Hock a Loogie from Beyond.*

WHILE SUPPLIES LAST!

THE FUTURE IS OVER

Jasper Dash, Boy Technonaut, was slumped on a couch. He and Lily were at his home of the future. It was a house made of concrete and plate glass and huge circular balconies and spiral staircases. It was supposed to be a home of the future, but it was now from a future that was far in the past. The Dashes' place had been designed and built many, many years before, so the concrete was cracking and the glass panels were sometimes streaked and fogged where water had gotten in between the panes. There was a weird smell in the upstairs closets that never went away.

Lily couldn't stand to see Jasper so upset. Normally, he wasn't like this. He usually didn't even notice setbacks, but strutted forward, eyes gleaming. He had been imprisoned in ice caves in Siberia and had been hung upside down in an Albanian gangster's lair. He had escaped diamond smugglers in the Congo and flesh-eating firemen on one of the moons of Saturn.*

"Jasper," said Lily, "I know it felt bad, but everyone's going to forget about it. They were laughing *with* you, not *at* you."

"I'm a fool," said Jasper. "The world has moved on past me."

"You're not a fool!" said Lily. "Who else in the school has invented an atomic-powered cellular telephone?"

"Nothing I do works out anymore. My hovering restaurant was hit by lightning. My mining ray caused the Halt 'n' Buy parking lot to collapse into a sinkhole. My flying Sky Suite fell and crushed a hotel in Delaware. My

---

* Which moon? Polydeuces, since you ask. See *Jasper Dash and His Remarkable Methane Mittens.*

rocket-powered car can't go faster than twenty-five miles per hour."

"Yes, it can!"

"I can't drive it anyway, because I'm still not old enough to have a license." Jasper turned over on his back. "I'm not *complaining*, Lily. I'm just saying I don't belong in this world anymore. I'm from a different time."

"We're calling Katie. She always knows how to cheer you up." Lily reached into her pocket to get her phone, then stopped herself. She didn't want to hurt his feelings. She pulled her hand out and pretended to fix her bangs. "Um, Jasper, do you maybe have a phone I could use?"

He looked at her with red-rimmed eyes. "Oh, just use the one in your pocket, Lily. It's no use trying to make me feel better." He flipped over onto his stomach. "Where is Katie, anyway?"

"Some Horror Hollow problem," said Lily. "Conjoined twin serial killers. She was really sorry she couldn't be here."

Katie Mulligan, like Jasper Dash, was the heroine of her own old book series. As you may have noticed, in the town of Pelt, there were many washed-up characters from old series, which was one of the reasons Lily loved living there. There were the Manley Boys, well-built sons of ace detective Bark Manley, who solved mysteries. There was that lovable pooch Terence, a hyper-intelligent cocker spaniel–poodle mix, who was always up to adorable mischief. There were some old, fat Photon Rangers who walked around in uniforms that looked like footie pajamas. And of course there were the Cutesy Dell Twins, two girls who always had crushes on hot guys and spent long hours asking each other, "I know he *likes* me—but does he, like, *like* like me?"

Katie Mulligan's series, Horrow Hollow, had first come out in the 1990s, and it featured Katie being haunted, kidnapped, threatened, chased, lifted, dangled, dropped, and almost burned alive by creepy enemies. But she gave as good as she got. Hardly a month went by when she wasn't slapping tiny little dragons with her flip-flop or reading spells backward to vanquish mean genies.

She was always there for her friends, though. She showed up pretty soon at Jasper's house, sweating from biking over and from fighting off the conjoined twin psychopaths.* She took off her winter coat and her hat. Her hair was flattened and smeared all over her forehead.

"Why, Katie, it's awfully kind of you to bike over," said Jasper. "How is it going with the conjoined serial killers?"

"Sorry I'm late!" said Katie. "It's been a tough mystery. Two sets of fingerprints, but only one set of footprints, you know?"

She scampered up the concrete stairs and playfully boxed with Jasper's limp arm. "What's happening, Jas?"

"I am done."

Katie blinked with surprise. "Whoa! What's

---

* In Horror Hollow #43: *Two Heads Are Badder Than One.*

wrong? Lily told me the science fair didn't go so good, but, uh . . . What about all your pluck and vim and vigor?"

Jasper slowly sat up. "My pluck has been plucked."

"What do you mean by 'done'?"

He said dismally, "When I began my adventures a long time ago, there were no computers. Airplanes were still new. Plastic was still thrilling. Astronomers had just discovered Pluto, the ninth and coldest planet in the solar system."

Katie plopped down next to him on the couch and slung her arm around his shoulders. "Um," she said, "hate to tell you, but Pluto: no longer a planet."

"What?"

"They de-made it a planet. They decided it wasn't planety enough. We only have eight again now."

"See?" groaned Jasper. "Do you know how proud the Plutonians were, the day I told them they had just been declared the ninth world in our solar system? There were parades in gratitude to all earthlings, and they made a statue of a human in one of their public parks. They showered it with confetti of ice that fell glinting in the starlight. They all gave speeches about unity and brotherhood and ate huge festival salads garnished with fungi from Yuggoth."

"Ja-a-a-a-a-asper!" Katie said, jerking her friend's whole body back and forth. "Snap out of it!"

"Everything I know is gone."

Lily asked him carefully, "What did you mean earlier when you said you were working on some kind of teleporter that would take people to the stars? Usually, you use rockets."

Katie added, "You like the roar."

Jasper shrugged. It looked like he didn't want to talk about it. He just said, "Oh . . . It was just an . . . idea I had. . . . Something I've been tinkering with . . . Nothing much."

Katie said, "Huh! You never mentioned it before."

Jasper looked down at their feet. "I just . . . I got the idea for it recently. In the middle of the night. You know, chums. Suddenly you wake up, and there's this whole idea in your head for an invention, and, *Eureka!* So I started building it. . . . It's really nothing. . . ."

"Wow," said Katie. "Can you just go anywhere? Instantly? And there, suddenly, you are, at the beach in California?"

Somewhat wearily, Jasper explained, "No. You have to have a teleporter booth to land in as well as one to send you. They send you back and forth."

"Isn't that kind of a pain?" Katie asked. "To have two booths?"

"Umm," Lily pointed out, "otherwise you wouldn't be able to get back. You'd appear on the beach in California and you'd have to drive back home."

"Good point," said Katie. "But how are

you going to find teleportation booths on other planets?"

Jasper didn't look right at them. "I don't know," he admitted. "I just . . . I had a dream, that if I built this teleporter booth . . . maybe there would be someone . . . who could . . . you know . . . receive me. I just felt like I had to . . . try it."

Lily said, "But you wouldn't go away to another planet without us, right? Your friends?"

Jasper smiled weakly. "Of course not, Lily," he said.

But he didn't look like he meant it.

Lily and Katie were worried about him. When it was time for dinner, they didn't go home. Lily whispered to Mrs. Dash, "Would you mind if we maybe could stay for dinner? Jasper's really upset, and we want to try to be here for him."

"Why, of course, honey," said Mrs. Dash. "Thank you for thinking of it. I'd be delighted."

They ate a solemn dinner, and then Katie

asked if they could hang out and watch a movie, but of course the only movies Jasper had at his house were old celluloid movies on huge reels. The movies had to be projected onto a screen. They watched a few from his collection.

That didn't help. There in black and white was Jasper Dash in 1942, looking just the same as he looked now, climbing into a plane and waving. There he was shutting the hatch on his Bullet Submersible. There he was playing Frisbee with a robot dog who had long since rusted.

Jasper's face fell as he watched the movies. Lily could tell he remembered what it was like back then when there was so much still to be explored and discovered in the world. She could tell he remembered what it was like to be inventing things, to be building, full of joy and hope in the future. And now the future had arrived and had passed, and it was over.

She and Katie were quiet when they left.

They said they'd see him in the morning.

In fact, they would not.

Jasper stared out the windows at the distant stars of the Milky Way. His breath spread and shrank on the plate glass.

His mother was watching him, leaning against a pillar.

"Jasper?" she said. "I know there are times we don't seem to fit in here."

Jasper nodded.

She asked him, "Is there anything I can do, honey?"

He didn't answer. He said, "Mother . . . What do you know about my father?"

"Who do you mean?"

"The one who sent the beam through space. From the region of the Horsehead Nebula."

"Do you think of that as your father, buttercup? It was just some alien."

"You never . . . met him . . . did you?"

"Of course not. And it might not have been a him or a her. I was just sitting at the observatory one night, looking through the telescope, when—goodness gracious me!—a tremendous beam of brilliant energy shot through the lens. My hair stuck straight out. Darling, I lit up like a chafing dish of flaming bananas Foster. I couldn't see a thing. My eyes were filled with ones and zeros." Dolores Dash crossed her arms. More quietly, she said, "When I woke up, everything was dark. I got up and went to tell the other astronomers what had happened. I slept on a cot right there at the laboratory so some of the medical scientists could keep an eye on me.

"In the morning, I got up, ate a full breakfast of eggs and bacon, and discovered that, well, I was still absolutely famished. I realized I wanted to drink specific chemicals, things I never would have thought of normally. Lots of them. I went down to the chemistry lab. I filled up test tubes with electrolytes and amino acids and powders and, goodness, who knows what all. I had very definite ideas. I kept mixing things up and drinking them down. They were delicious. I just knew what to do because of that beam of energy. And somehow, Jasper . . . my boy . . . my perfect, special boy . . . somehow, all those swizzled acids turned into you." She smiled at him and held out her hand for him to take it. "Jasper?" she said.

He frowned and focused on the carpet.

"I'm sorry, Jasper. I'm sorry we're alone. Is there anything I can do?"

He shook his head. "I'm going up to my laboratory," he said.

She tried to make conversation. "What are you working on?"

"A transporter . . . to take people to other stars."

"No jet rockets?"

"No rockets. It's just an instant and then you're there. If it works."

"Of course you won't use it without permission, honey."

"No, Mom."

He trudged to the staircase.

He stopped just before he went up. He

thought for a while, and then he asked Mrs. Dash, "Do you think my father will ever come to get me?"

Jasper's mother went to him. She enfolded her son in her arms. But he didn't move or relax. He stood perfectly still, like he was waiting for her to stop.

She gave up hugging him and let go. Without saying anything else, he went up the stairs.

He dragged himself to his bedroom and sat down at his desk. It was covered with the plans for his Astounding Atomic Telephone Cart. He had left them there in excitement that morning, before the disastrous science fair.

In a sudden fury, he grabbed those plans and crumpled them. He tore at them. He couldn't make the pieces small enough. He flung the blueprints at the wastebasket.

It was extremely unusual for Jasper to get angry, except at injustice and gangsters. This was perhaps the first time in all his ninety years of being thirteen that he had ever had a tantrum.

He sat with his elbows on his desk. Then, picking up a soldering gun, he went over to his transporter booth. It was almost finished.

He was squatting next to it, wearing magnifying goggles, when his mother knocked quietly at the door.

"Hi there, Mom," he said.

She took one look at the booth he was working on and its huge metal projections. Then she said with some irritation in her voice, "Jasper Dash, is that your instantaneous teleporter?"

Jasper nodded. "Yes, Mother."

"What are you planning to do with it?"

Jasper wouldn't answer. He just shrugged.

His mother put her hands on her hips. "I'm only going to ask this once," she said, "and I want a real answer. Are you thinking of transporting yourself to the space coordinates in the region of the Horsehead Nebula where that beam came from that created you?"

Jasper didn't answer. He wouldn't tell a lie.

"No!" said his mother. "No, and no, and

for the last time, no. Really, honey. I let you do a lot of things. But a parent has to put her foot down somewhere."

"Mother!"

"And I put my foot down when it comes to interstellar travel. You are absolutely *not* going to project yourself into the middle of a purple cloud of interstellar gas, and that's *final*! Is that understood, Jasper?"

He stood up defiantly. "It's what I've always wanted to do! This is what I've wanted for years, Mother! And I just figured out the secret to the teleporter a couple of weeks ago! I want to—"

"I said *NO*, Jasper! No Horsehead Nebula!"

"Please!"

"Jasper Augustus Dash, I think I've been pretty understanding over the years. I never complained about you going to the center of the Earth. I never said a word about you fighting the ninjas in their secret assassins' lair. I never told you that you weren't allowed to

build a deep-sea observation bubble in the Mariana Trench. And I said you could go out past Neptune as long as you stayed in the solar system and loaded the dishwasher first. But this—it's crazy, Jasper. You don't know what's out there! So no. No, no, no."

Jasper glared at his mother. For the first time in his life, he was furious at someone who loved him. For the first time ever, he was tired of being good and heroic and polite to his elders. He stood up and faced her.

"Don't start, Jasper," she said, holding out a warning finger. "Or do I have to confiscate your atom-smasher?"

"FINE!" he yelled. *"FINE!"*

Mrs. Dash was shocked. Jasper had never yelled at her before, except maybe things like, "WATCH OUT!" when a robot with machine-gun hands was firing through the kitchen windows.

In a tone she had never used before, Mrs. Dash said, "Sometimes, Jasper, I wish you *did* have a father to help me take care of you."

Icily, he replied, "Sometimes, Mother, so—do—I."

She turned white with shock. Then she stormed out, slamming the door behind her.

Jasper's hands were shaking. He wanted to go apologize. He didn't know what had come over him. He hated how he was being. He didn't understand it. He'd never been this way before.

He sat down next to the teleportation booth. He pouted. Then he picked up a wrench and went back to work. He'd show her.

As Mrs. Dash lay in her bed, she thought about her son. She never wanted him to be hurt. Of course he'd be hurt sometimes—a bruise under the eye from secret agents, a leg broken by the yeti—but she never wanted him to lose his hope in the future. She decided that in the morning, she would apologize. She would explain herself better. She would warn him that finding his father might not be as easy as he thought. She would do it at breakfast, over pancakes.

She went to sleep, knowing she'd try her best to prepare him for the difficult road ahead. Maybe she would actually go with him in his teleporter. They could appear together, hand in hand, on some alien world to greet the being who had sent the instructions on how to grow Jasper. It could be a family trip. . . .

Dolores Dash fell asleep. She did not notice that at about three o'clock, her night-light dimmed, as if something in the house was using all the power.

The concrete house of the future was silent.

Outside, wind blew across the snowbanks and through the dead briars.

In the morning, when she went to wake her son for pancakes, he was gone.

What a Wonderful World

Earlier that same night, in the state of Michigan, a couple of teenagers out on a date were abducted by a flying saucer.

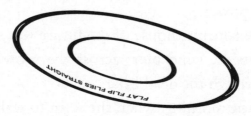

FLAT FLIP FLIES STRAIGHT

For a month since the family Delb had been stolen away on a cold January night in the middle of a prologue, there had been saucer sightings across North America. They always happened in remote, strange places. You know how it is with aliens. Even though they're supposed to want to make contact with our odd, half-hairy species and give us messages, they never just land in the middle of a city with a big crowd watching and step out of their ships waving their claws like the Queen of England. No, they always make contact with people in empty, desolate, out-of-the-way locations:

☞ Flat farms in the Midwest. Nothing but the green of the fields and the white beam from the lightly bobbing ship up above.

☞ Cabins in the woods. The knobs on all the doors start turning at once.

☞ High up in the cold air above Alaska. An air force pilot turns and sees a disk heading right toward him.

☞ The red desert, with a green evening sky. No town for miles. Electrical towers strung together by wires stand across the horizon like an alien army with their arms spread wide. They are motionless in the evening, the wires singing. Far off, a glint of silver light appears.

☞ Swamps where men in rubber pants fish at twilight. There is a glow under the water. The pond starts to boil. Something rises out of it. Something bigger than a house, with water streaming off its metal hide. The men stumble backward. They will never be able to make it through the woods to the road. They will never make it.

Alien abduction is part of the American poetry of loneliness.

Young Jed Lostrup did not think it was going to be a lonely night. Nope. On the contrary. Jed got off work at the warehouse and drove to pick up his date. She was a girl called Shirley. He had been wanting to go on a date with her forever. Since the beginning of high school. Finally he got the guts to ask her out when they were both chosen to sing solos with the high school choir.

He had to rush to make it to her house on time after work. He rolled along the highway as fast as he could. He got off at her exit. He screeched to a halt in front of her house and ran across the lawn, straightening his shirt. He rang the bell.

There she was. He couldn't believe it. His dream. She looked beautiful in her sweater, with her hair.

"Hi," they said awkwardly.

He said, "You ready, Shirley?"

She looked up and down the street. "Where's, um, where's your car, Jed?"

"Oh," he said sheepishly. "I came right from work. I don't have a car. I don't own one."

"So you came to pick me up," she clarified, "in a *forklift*?"

"Yeah. Brought the forklift from work."

Shirley smiled weakly, like someone who was about to make an excuse. "Oh. Great."

"Come on, Shirl, just wait till you see this baby go!"

She held on to the door frame like it was something that floated and she was something that sank. "I don't know . . . ," she said. "Maybe sometime when you . . . have . . . a . . . you know. Car."

"Come *on*." He knew it was crazy, but he grabbed her wrist and pulled her out across the lawn. "I got it set up all special."

He was not just talking about the fact that he had hung a mesquite air freshener in the cab of the forklift. Also, on the lifting forks, there was a . . .

Shirley said, "Is that an upright piano?"

"Yup!" He smiled proudly. "And not just any upright piano. A *player* piano. I wanted to make it romantic."

He ran over to the forklift and climbed in. He started up the engine. It growled loudly. Then he pulled on a string, and the player piano started to hammer out "Some Enchanted Evening."

Jed's grin was so wide that Shirley couldn't help smiling too. And then she started laughing. And then they both were laughing. And he held out a hand like a gentleman and helped her into the forklift. They puttered along through the suburbs with the player piano tinkling and banging away. People looked out their windows in astonishment. Jed put his foot on the gas, and they got up to ten miles per hour.

And it was, indeed, some enchanted evening, at first. They went to a J. P. Barnigan's American Family Restaurant on the highway and they had as many waffle fries as a person could eat. They talked and found they had a lot in common. They made jokes about their choir director. The room was decorated with brass railings and old rowing oars and sports team photos and a shelf of dusty Jasper Dash books.

"It's so sad!" said Shirley. "I bet no one ever reads these books anymore." She lifted one down from the shelf. She and Jed took turns reading from it while they waited for the bill. They loved all the corny old exclamations like "Jupiter's moons!" and "By gum!"

Jed was driving faster on the way home than on the way out. (There were free refills on Coke, and he'd had about seven.) It was a forklift, so that still only meant about fifteen miles per hour. But anyway, that was probably why he got off at the wrong exit.

They were a little lost.

They were driving along beside what was a

cornfield in the summer. Now the stalks were all broken up and black. The trees were black too, and the road was black, and the sky was black and stormy. They didn't mind, though. Shirley had very carefully started to lean against Jed, and the piano was playing "What a Wonderful World."

Jed looked around. "Oh, shoot, Shirley. We're lost. At ten miles per hour."

He started to turn around in a field.

They bumbled back along the dark road.

Shirley asked, "What do you think the other kids in the choir would say if they knew we went on a—" Then she stopped.

There was something in the road.

Some *one*.

Caught in the forklift's headlights.

A figure standing perfectly still in the middle of the road.

Outlined in black: a humanoid shape, but too thin and spindly to be a person, wearing a helmet with fins.

And then Jed looked to the side and saw that, in the middle of the field, there was a great white saucer sitting darkly, and he began screaming.

He struggled to turn the forklift around. The dark, tall figure walked toward them. The piano played "I Don't Want to Set the World on Fire."

Jed put his foot to the floor. The forklift trundled off the road and into the field. Its tractor wheels half sank in mud. Now it was going even slower. Jed didn't pay attention. He leaned forward against the wind.

"Don't you worry, Shirley! I'll get us out of— Hold on!"

She held on to his arm as they went over bumps and troughs.

"Look back!" Jed shouted over the engine. "How we doing?"

Shirley swiveled her head.

The alien walked beside them at his own pace. He slowed down sometimes so he wouldn't get ahead of them.

"Um," she said.

The alien raised a glass wand.

There was a beeping sound in their ears.

And then they both fell asleep.

* * *

The frozen cornfield was empty except for an abandoned forklift.

A player piano on the front of it sadly and slowly played a song:

> *Blue moon,*
> *You saw me standing alone . . .*

* * *

The interrogation was terrifying. Brilliant white light. Weightlessness. Tumbling through the air.

"WHERE IS JASPER DASH?"

"WHERE IS THE HUMAN NAMED JASPER DASH?"

"IF YOU REMAIN SILENT ANY LONGER, YOU WILL BE SORRY!"

"YOUR WHOLE WORLD WILL SUFFER FOR YOUR SILENCE!"

All these voices screaming—until finally Shirley shouted back, "All right! All right! You don't have to yell! He's from—he's from some stupid

old books that no one even reads anymore!* The
books say he lives in a town called Pelt!"

---

* This is not strictly true. You, after all, have a stack of the Jasper Dash
books that you got at the church rummage sale. A couple of days later, the
woman who owns the vacation house your family rented comes by to see
if everything's okay, and she sees the books and laughs. She says that the
Jasper Dash books were in the house for years, and that they just gave them
to the church rummage sale a few weeks ago to get rid of them.

She says, "Here they are back again. Like a bad penny!"

That is a weird coincidence. I don't need to tell you this, but you think,
*That's really crazy. Maybe there's something cosmic in it. Like the books
just belong in this house.*

So one afternoon when your brother and a cousin are hogging the computer, you go up to the bedroom where all the kids sleep, even your annoy-
ing cousin Maxwell, who snores like a lumber mill. You reach under your
bed and go through your duffel bag and take out *Jasper Dash and His Marvelous Electro-Neutron Sled.*

Sitting under a tree by the lake, you open it up. You begin to read.

What's it about? The Alaskan wilderness . . . a wild search for an old
sailing ship trapped in the ice a century earlier . . . Supposedly, there are
priceless paintings still onboard . . . and Jasper Dash is whamming across
the tundra in his Electro-Neutron Sled, seeking the lost treasure ship, rac-
ing against time and thugs. Every chapter ends with a cliffhanger: a shoot-
out or a polar bear or a snow avalanche or a bomb. When you look up, it is
almost evening. Your father is grilling things.

You wonder who the books used to belong to. You flip through the
pages. On the inside of the front cover, someone, a long time ago, has written, "Busby Spence" in awkward letters. Then they wrote, "1942."

You wonder who Busby Spence was, and you feel a ghostly shiver come
over you. These books were originally from this house. You wonder what
Busby Spence was like. You wonder whether he read this same book sitting
in this yard, under this tree, by this lake.

Slowly you reach down with a finger and touch his name. It is like you
are touching him through time, through a pane of glass.

Busby Spence. He wrote his name there so long ago, he is probably a
grandfather now, an old man, or dead.

The lights shut off.

Shirley and Jed fell back asleep.

They awoke in a field.

It was morning. Steam was coming off the cold ground. Broken cornstalks lay around them.

Far away, the spaceship was headed for Pelt.

Gone!

But Jasper had not been kidnapped from his bedroom by an alien spaceship.

That was the first possibility his mother thought of. (It had happened before.)

She frantically ran to the teleporter booth. The door of the booth was shut. A green light was on.

She gasped and stumbled backward.

Jasper had finished making his machine and had used it.

She quickly looked at the dials that set the coordinates for teleportation.

She put her hand over her mouth.

Her worst nightmare had come true: Jasper had teleported himself to the region of the Horsehead Nebula.

FAMILY VACATION

A million particles of Jasper Dash shot across the galaxy like a thousand tiny bubbles flurrying through a soda straw.

Pancakes, Peril, and Panic

Mrs. Dash stumbled back downstairs to the breakfast nook. She threw herself unsteadily down onto a chair, gasping. She clutched at her own robe. She looked down at the breakfast she had made her son. Here were his pancakes, still warm—and he was perhaps farther away from home than any human being had ever been.

She prayed that he was safely on his way to the Horsehead Nebula, and that he would still be safe once he got there.

She prayed that he would not be too horrified by what he found there, whatever it was. Because she knew this: Just because a thing sends a highly concentrated beam of information to a distant world to build a genius son doesn't mean that it will be a father. It doesn't mean that it will be kind or that it will care at all.

There are many reasons to send highly concentrated beams of information to distant worlds.

Mrs. Dash had known this day would come.

Jasper's pancakes sat uneaten. His grapefruit was sliced in half. Beside his plate was his favorite breakfast drink: Choco-Vanilla Flavor Gargletine™ ("It's Pep in a Pop-Top Can!").*

---

* Gargletine™ Breakfast Drink comes in many thrilling, gob-smackin' flavors, including Chocolate, Banana, Lemon, and new Pork Cracklin' Delight. For many years in the late 1930s, on Jasper Dash's radio program, a quartet of singers sang advertisements for Gargletine with jingles like,

"Wanna wash your innards clean?
Keep your kidneys peachy-keen?
Daily, gulp your GARGLETINE!"

In old advertisements, there were pictures of Jasper firing off his laser with one hand while stirring up a delicious mug of Gargletine Breakfast Drink with the other.

Busby Spence, the boy whose name was written in your Jasper Dash books, used to drink a thick, bubbling glass of Gargletine every morning. Then, in 1941, when Busby was ten years old, America entered the Second World War. Quickly, production of Gargletine was stopped. Its ingredients were needed by the government to make bombs.

Busby's father went away to war.

But Jasper Dash would not be home for breakfast.

Busby read his Jasper Dash books under a tree, waiting for his father to come home.

Far out at sea, planes dropped bombs on enemy ships. As the bombs fell, the pilots sang:

"Axis powers acting mean?
Think you see a submarine?
Blow 'em up with GARGLETINE!"

SOME PICNIC

Jasper Dash, Boy Technonaut, woke up to find himself in the region of the Horsehead Nebula. He was on the third planet circling a star called Zeblion.

He was in a booth that looked almost exactly like his teleporter at home, except much bigger.

He adjusted the helmet of his space suit. He stood up slowly. Teleportation had made him kind of tired and headachy. He figured his blood must have gone the wrong way.

He opened the door and stepped out.

The Boy Technonaut stared in astonishment. He gasped.

Jasper Dash stood in a big stone room. In front of him was a welcome party that someone

65

had prepared for him many, many years before. It was now all decayed. There was a futuristic picnic table with paper plates. The plates had pictures of balloons and rockets on them. There was dead confetti on the floor. Overhead, some cardboard letters on a string, partially fallen, spelled out,

WELCOME HOME JA
S
P
E
R

D
ASH!!!

Jasper went over to the table. There was the remains of a cake. There were streamers.

Gently Jasper picked up a noisemaker. The top of it was gray with dust. He wiped it on his space suit and brought it up toward his face to blow through it. It clacked against his helmet. He detached his air hose and stuck the noise-maker onto the end of it.

A lonely razz echoed through the cold stone room. The noisemaker uncurled unwillingly like the head of a geriatric turtle.

Jasper reattached his air hose to his helmet and put the noisemaker in one of his pockets.

He looked over the ruins of his party. *His* party. Someone had set up a party *just for him*. Many decades ago, but still: a party.

He was furious at his mother. He couldn't believe that she had tried to stop him from coming. He was glad he had disobeyed her for the first time in his life.

He wondered who the other guests would have been. Who had waited for him? Who had expected him? Who had been disappointed when he didn't come?

He blinked back tears.

No time for that.

He looked around the room. Other than

the defunct party and the teleporter, there was nothing in the room.

He inspected the teleporter. Even though it was bigger than his, it looked very similar. Very, very similar.

Jasper Dash started to wonder if he had really made up the plan for the teleporter entirely by himself. After all, he had dreamed it. He had thought of the secret of teleportation one night when he was half-asleep. Maybe (he realized) it was not his idea. Maybe it had come from space, like the beam that had created him. Maybe it was not a dream.

Maybe it had been broadcast to him by someone else.

Maybe by a father who wanted to meet him.

It was time to explore.

He walked over to the exit. It was a metal door.

He opened it.

And alarms went off.

Jasper stumbled back. The walls were flashing. There was a whooping.

Jasper grabbed his ray gun, just in case.

Then all the noise stopped. The alarms shut down.

Jasper wondered who the alarms had warned of his arrival.

The door stood open.

A quiet breeze came in from outside.

Jasper stepped out for his first view of the Horsehead Nebula.

* * *

He had not known what to bring with him on his expedition. He had packed quickly at three in the morning. He had certainly not prepared for a party.

In his backpack and his utility belt were:

- his ray gun (already mentioned)
- a flashlight
- a galactic compass
- a Swiss Army knife
- stacks of sandwiches
  - five peanut butter and jelly
  - three turkey and cranberry sauce
  - two bologna and cheese
  - all of them liquefied for easy slurping
- a toothpaste tube of curly fries
- two jars of Gargletine™ Brand Breakfast Drink—"It's Zap in a Syrup!"
- a package of dehydrated water pills ("Just add water!")
- a canteen of water
- salt for the curly fries

Jasper, a lone figure on a weird world, stood against the violet sky.

The building where he had landed towered above him. Most of it was a giant antenna of some kind. It looked more like a growth.

Above it, space was filled with billows and swells and trails of scarlet gas and dust, all of it lit by the glare from birthing stars. Black streamers tiger-striped the dome of heaven.

Jasper blinked up at the beauty of the view.

The horizon was made up of tall, knobby mountains of dull green glass. Their peaks were steep and curved, like the mountains in old Chinese paintings. Natural bridges of stone led between them, hanging over huge chasms and gulfs.

On different hilltops, Jasper saw other buildings with other antennas like the one behind him.

The Boy Technonaut didn't know which way to go. He just started walking.

* * *

In about two hours, he arrived at another one of the antennas. He found that the stone building beneath the antenna was collapsing. Part of the wall had fallen down.

He went in, shining his flashlight. He stepped over huge chunks of alien rock.

There was nothing there but crushed blobs.

At first he was afraid they might originally have been friendly blobs. He nudged them. Then he decided they hadn't been nice blobs at all, or mean blobs, or any kind of blob that moved around and talked. They had been something else. Maybe furniture. Like beanbag chairs, he thought.

He saw, in the corner, another teleporter machine. It was dusty and unused.

As he stepped back out of the fallen chamber into the purple twilight, he looked at the other antennas that were silhouetted on the horizon. He was starting to suspect that each one was a station that originally sent people to and from a different planet. He wondered who had built them.

He hiked to the next one. It was also empty, except for some dry slime.

He kept on going. Hours passed.

He got to the next antenna. This one was different. There was a web of wires coming out of the building, tangled and glittering. They were fixed on broken pillars of rock.

He wondered what the network was. He went up to it and examined it. He took one of the wires between his fingers. He figured it was copper. Just a guess. He had once had quite a bit of experience with metal scrap.*

———————————

* During World War II, Jasper appeared in a series of comic strips telling kids about how they and everyone else could help the US Army by bringing in junk metal to be turned into Jeeps and tanks. There was Jasper's shiny, smiling face and his thumbs-up next to a caption that read,

> What's more fun, kids, than exploring dinosaur forests at the earth's core or fighting electrical space pirates? How about searching old, abandoned houses and mine shafts for **SCRAP?**
>
> That's right! Uncle Sam needs you to hunt for junk metal and other refuse! Play your part in the War Effort! Even cooking grease can be used for explosives!
> Remember . . .
>
> > 100 silk stockings . . . make . . . 1 parachute
> > 1 garden hose . . . makes . . . 1 life raft

He squinted at the ruined building, but decided he didn't want to go in yet. It was time for a rest. He sat on a boulder, took out a sandwich, and drank it.

Giant space spiders, he thought grimly, looking at the web. *It would be nice if just this once, there were no giant space spiders.* He hoped that

---

2 inner tubes . . . make . . . 3 gas masks
I Family car . . . makes . . . 26 machine guns
18 tin cans . . . make . . . I portable Flamethrower
So head up to your attics and down to your basements and scamper into your neighbor's yard!

GET IN THE SCRAP!
SALVAGE for VICTORY!

Busby Spence, one of Jasper Dash's greatest fans, read these comics while the spring rain fell outside the screened-in porch. He and his mother loaded their neighbor's truck up with junk.

A few months later, when the summer came, he wondered about the junk and what the army had made out of it. Just the year before, he'd floated on the lake with those old rubber inner tubes, suspended between the blue sky and the blue water. Everything had been silent. It was strange to think that now those inner tubes were maybe worn as a gas mask on the face of some soldier crouched in a trench in the midst of howling sandstorms and shelling. Golf clubs were guns. Old bicycles were bullets. Everything had changed. He pictured his mother's silk stockings billowing in the upper air, spreading into parachutes, and men suspended from the dainty feet, surveying the enemy's fields below.

He hoped his father, wherever he was, would be proud of what they'd found and saved.

was not too much to ask. He was tired of giant space spiders, tired of being spun into a bundle and having to cut his way out and then—then!—the boring laser battle and all the chittering. He took a solemn sip of his bologna and cheese.

He looked at the broken antennas ranged throughout the mountains beneath the weird, glaring sky. No one was here. He could feel the emptiness. He had come so many millions of miles across the galaxy, hoping for so much, and now there was nobody to greet him. No one to mess up his hair with a hand and say, "Well done, Jas! Just think of you inventing a matter transporter that instantaneously teleports anything fifteen hundred light-years through interstellar space to the planet Zeblion III in the region of the Horsehead Nebula!" No one to tell him why they had sent a highly concentrated beam of binary information to the planet Earth in the first place and inspired Jasper's mother to glug rare chemicals. No one at all.

The planet was dead. The civilization that had built him was dead.

No—no! He would not give up. He could not face going back home to his house and admitting to his mom that there was no one on Zeblion III. She would coo at him and say, "Oh, I'm so sorry, darling, so sorry, honeykins," and pet him like a cat and it would be awful.

He got angry just thinking about her. How she never talked about where he came from. How she hardly ever even talked about the highly concentrated beam of binary information projected from the region of the Horsehead Nebula.

Jasper Dash was more determined than ever: He was going to reappear in that teleporter with his secret alien father at his side.

The swirls in the sky burned over his head. He craned his neck and tried to admire the view. He wished there was someone there to share it. Lily and Katie, maybe. Certainly not his mom.

But in fact, someone was there with him.

It was someone with plans.

Jasper heard a staticky shout. He looked up.

A spark jolted out of the wires near Jasper's head, zapping to the boy's helmet, sending shocks all through his body. The Boy Technonaut leaped and juddered in pain.

Jasper Dash lay on the green, glassy mountainside beneath the tangle of wires.

Electrical shocks crackled up and down his space suit.

As he passed out, his last waking thought was, *Some picnic.*

"Thank you girls for coming over and helping me look for Jasper," said Mrs. Dash, when Lily and Katie got into her car. "I am absolutely frantic."

"No probs, Mrs. Dash," said Katie, slamming the door shut. "Where did you say you think he's gone?"

Dolores Dash answered, "The region of the Horsehead Nebula," and she hit the gas.

Lily said quietly, "To find his dad?"

"Oh . . . ," said Mrs. Dash, disgusted. "His *dad*."

"How do you know he went to the Horsehead Nebula?" Katie asked.

"The coordinates on his new teleporter. And when I found out he was missing, I ran down to the garage. He took his space suit with him. He wouldn't have had time to go get it if he'd been abducted from his room." She put her red thumbnail between her teeth and bit it in worry. "I'm sorry, girls," she said. "I don't mean to startle you. We could talk about something pleasanter. How are things with you? Katie, how are your serial killer conjoined twins?"

Katie rolled her eyes. "Fine. It turned out one twin was good and one was evil, so they're duking it out right now at a gymnastics class. I hope the good one wins."

"It must be very difficult for you, over in Horror Hollow."

Katie shrugged. "No worse than for you and Jasper. I can't believe him, taking off without us. He's kind of a jerk. I mean, a jerk I totally love, but a jerk."

Lily said, "How are we going to find him? Do we have to follow him to the Horsehead Nebula?"

Mrs. Dash sighed. "I don't know, Lily. That's the problem. I really don't know."

She screeched into her garage of the future and hit a button on her dashboard. A robotic hand snaked out and pulled the garage door shut behind them.

As she got out of the car, Mrs. Dash took off her sunglasses and head scarf. "Look," she said sentimentally, pointing to a pegboard. "That's where my little boy usually hangs his interplanetary pressure suit. And that's where he plugs in his Pneumatic Air Recycler to recharge it. He even took his own *air* with him." Close to tears, she wailed, "What kind of mother am I, girls? What kind of mother lets her own son go off alone to someplace where there's not even any *oxygen*?"

She shook her head, and they went upstairs.

As they walked through the glassed-in living room, Katie looked out the window and saw a dog running over the snow toward the house.

"Look at that cute dog out on your lawn!" said Katie. "Is it the neighbor's?"

Mrs. Dash squinted. "Oh, that's Terence, the mischievous, hyperintelligent dog from next door."

The dog was barking viciously at nothing.

Katie asked, "What kind of a dog is he?"

"A poodle–cocker spaniel mix. Whatever that's called. A cocker-doodle."

The dog growled at nothing, or maybe at something on the roof. Anyway, he started backing up and whining.

Katie said, "He looks really smart. But he's acting weird. What's wrong with him?"

Mrs. Dash waved her hand in the air. "Who knows? He usually only acts like that when something terrifying and alien is invading."

Katie exclaimed, "He's super cute, even when he's barking at the unknown."

"He's not so cute when he leaves messes all over your lawn. I am tired of waking up at dawn every morning to a cocker-doodle doo. Come along, girls. I'll show you the teleporter machine."

They continued up the stairs.

Out on the white, snowy lawn, Terence the cocker-doodle backed away from the Dashes' house of the future, growling and whimpering.

Like I said: as if there was something alien on the roof.

* * *

Lily, Katie, and Mrs. Dash stood in Jasper's dimly lit bedroom laboratory. They were inspecting the teleporter. Mrs. Dash said, "Jasper told me that it teleports you to a similar machine on another world. He just had a hunch there was a receiving station where that beam came from, in the region of the Horsehead Nebula." She sighed. "A *hunch*. My little boy is fifteen hundred light-years away because of a *hunch*. What if there *was* no receiving station there? What if there was nothing? What if his molecules just . . . you know . . . scattered? He might not even *exist* anymore!"

Katie took her wrist. "Mrs. Dash, Jasper wouldn't do something stupid. He's never been stupid in his whole life. Don't worry."

Lily said, "The green light is on. So that must mean that something worked." She examined the machine. She could see in a little window. "There's a lever in there so you can work it from inside. It's pushed to 'Teleport.'"

"Yes, Lily," said Mrs. Dash. "Yes, see, he must have sent himself away. And look. These dials here have the spatial coordinates for Zeblion III, a planet near the Horsehead Nebula."

"So why don't we just follow him?" Katie said.

"Oh, that would be frightfully dangerous," said Mrs. Dash. "For one thing, he was wearing a space suit when he went. There probably isn't even any *atmosphere* where he is."

"No probs," said Katie enthusiastically. "He made Lily and me space suits once for a picnic on Jupiter. There sure is a lot of gravity there. The sandwiches were totally smooshed."*

Katie slid open one of Jasper's closets. She rummaged through all the gadgets.

Mrs. Dash thought hard. "Yes . . . And I have a suit left over from when I was an astronomer. . . . Somewhere . . . I remember it had a darling little skirt to it. . . . But really, we'd have to phone your

---

* In Jasper Dash #113: *Jasper Dash and the Gas Giant Picnic.*

parents first before we go to a nebula. Katie, your father is still cross with me from the time I took you to Santa's Christmas Fun World and you lost your dental retainer. So I think interstellar travel would be out of the question."

"Ta-da!" said Katie, and pulled two space suits out of the closet.

Lily was just starting to say, "Katie, I'm not sure we should just—" when they all stopped still.

There was a noise from Mrs. Dash's bedroom. A crash. A clatter. Breaking glass. Crunching.

Dolores Dash, Lily, and Katie looked at one another wildly.

Something had just burst through the window in the other room.

They strained to hear more. There was no sound.

Mrs. Dash hissed, "Curse that wall-to-wall carpeting."

Down the hall, something surveyed Mrs. Dash's bedroom. It found nothing of interest there. A bed. A nightstand. A lamp. A closet, full of clothes. The alien being moved to the door. It turned the knob.

It made its way down the hall.

Its footfalls were slow and deliberate.

It came to Jasper's room. It opened the door. It walked in.

It saw all the experiments laid out on benches and frames and brackets. It walked to the teleporter machine. It examined the dials and the cranks.

Then it turned.

There was a frigid breeze in the room. The alien being looked at the bedroom window.*

---

* Through the window in your bedroom at the vacation house, Busby Spence used to stare up at the stars each night. He saw outer space above the pines.

In one of those huge old pines you see, Busby and his father built a tree house. Busby's father sawed the wood, singing funny songs. He and Busby banged in the nails together. It was a great tree house with a deck and a rope swing and everything. You could jump off the rope-swing into the lake. All the kids from the neighborhood met at the tree house to read comics and talk about their baseball games.

During the war, Busby Spence and his friend Harmon stopped using the tree house. This was because in the summer of 1942 it was completely taken over by a mean, sloppy gang of raccoons.

Busby and Harmon tried to get the raccoons out of the tree house by

The window was open.

It went to look out.

There was a rope ladder leading down from

---

banging on the floor from below with a stick. Then they tried throwing rocks in the window. The raccoons didn't budge.

So Harmon and Busby tried to hold a meeting in the tree house anyway. They sat in one corner and the raccoons sat in the other corner. Busby read out the Order of Business in a loud, firm voice.

The raccoons stared at Busby and Harmon, and Busby and Harmon stared back.

It was a short, loud meeting and was followed by a trip to the doctor and lots of shots and stitches.

Finally Busby and Harmon built a new tree house. The second tree house was not as good as the first tree house. Busby's father wasn't around to help. He was great at building things—very careful and precise—and Busby wasn't. Busby wished his father was there to teach him how to measure and cut everything right. None of the boards in the second tree house fit, and the whole thing wobbled. From the second tree house Busby and Harmon could occasionally see the raccoons lying on their backs and relaxing on the porch of the first tree house.

Sometimes Busby and Harmon used the second tree house as a base to attack the raccoon thugs in the first tree house. And when Harmon and Busby left food in the second tree house, the gang of raccoons invaded at night and stole it, lugging it back to the first tree house. The raccoons would eat the food sitting on the porch, in full view. Then Busby and Harmon would huck pinecones. Then the raccoons would make a kind of scary laughing noise. Things went back and forth.

This went on for many months. It was one of the lesser-known battles of the Second World War.

Now, in a new century, you look out through those pines at the lake and the dark hills. The snoring of your cousin Maxwell rattles the walls. The tree houses are gone, and have been gone for two generations. You stare at the stars.

Nights pass in your life too.

the window. There was one pair—and only one pair—of human footprints in the snow, leading into the forest.

It turned suspiciously and looked around the room.

HUNTED BY WHATEVER-IT-IS

Katie and Lily crouched down on the floor of the teleporter booth, clutching their space suits. They were back to back, heads ducked. The shadow of something moving outside the booth fell across them.

They scrunched down as far as they could. Lily closed her eyes.

She heard the slow padding of alien feet across the carpet.

She clenched her fists. She could feel Katie's back sweating.

They heard the footsteps moving to the window. The thing, whatever it was, paused.

In those final few seconds before whatever-it-was had burst into the room, Mrs. Dash had opened the window and hissed to the girls, "Hide! I'll draw him out into the woods!" The girls had looked hurriedly around the room—then they'd stuffed themselves into the teleportation booth.

Everything depended on the monster following the obvious escape route out the window.

Lily held her breath.

Katie prayed, *Be interested in the outdoors. Be interested in the outdoors. Be interested in the outdoors.*

But whatever it was, it was not interested in snow-covered lawns or forested areas.

The footsteps came toward the booth.

Katie and Lily crushed themselves down toward the floor. Lily put her face between her knees. But now her eyes were open.

So she could see, in the window of the booth, the hideous head appear.

A goggly, finned alien helmet peered down at them. She could see it grab the handle of the door . . .

. . . and start to pull.

GONE IN A FLASH

Lily screeched—a high-pitched yip she was embarrassed by later.

She reached out her hand and pulled a big lever—the biggest.

There weren't many to pull.

Everything swam in front of her eyes. She saw the space monster struggling to open the door. She saw Katie turn toward her in horror . . . and then everything vanished.

They sifted down to their atoms—flung through space.

Across the arcs of a thousand suns.

Past worlds with rocky deserts and worlds with purple gardens.

Deep into the heart of the Horsehead Nebula.

* * *

The alien reeled backward in surprise. The humans were gone.

It quickly inspected the teleporter machine. It ran its hands over the controls.

It would not follow the humans. That would be foolish. They went to certain destruction.

It went to the window. It would follow the other human's footprints through the fallen, frozen water, into the scraggly black growths.

It had many ways of finding what it needed to find.

It began clumsily climbing down the rope ladder to the snow.

JOG WITH ALIENS

Through the woods ran Dolores Dash, her breath shooting out as steam.

She could hear something crashing and walking steadily toward her.

There were six square miles of forest behind Jasper Dash's house, filled with bunkers from all his old experiments and even the entrance to a tunnel that led to the center of the Earth.* Now Mrs. Dash knew she had to get the monster lost in those six square miles, because she had to keep it from going back to the house and finding the

---

* It was no longer accessible. The Boy Technonaut had dynamited it closed long ago to keep the pale, sightless dinosaurs of the nether regions from stampeding through the world up above. See *Jasper Dash in the Court of the Fungus Lords.*

girls—wherever they were hiding. (She didn't know they'd already thrown themselves fifteen hundred light-years away and would be very hard to find.) So Mrs. Dash jogged through the woods, trying to make as much noise as possible.

Now, you know as well as I do what usually happens in movies when women of the mid-twentieth century are chased through the woods by alien monsters: They trip on a branch and fall down. Then they lie there with their blond hair and their slim, scarlet-nailed fingers half covering their eyes until *whatever is chasing them* suddenly appears. . . . Their blue eyes widen . . . **ROAR!** . . . end of scene.

Mrs. Dash was just not interested in any of that happening. She had been on the cross-country running team back in high school and college. She knew the paths through the woods like the backs of her slim, scarlet-nailed hands. So she ran like the dickens.

She jumped over branches.

Behind her, she heard the monster trip and fall.

It lay there, looking at her through its finned helmet and its slim, silver-gloved hands. It struggled to its feet and kept running after her.

There were acres and acres of trees and snow and ice and shivery wind.

She leaped over a ditch.

The monster fell again.

Ha, she thought. *I haven't lost it since I ran the mile against Amoskeag Junior Women's College.*

She turned a corner.

And there were three aliens there.

They were too skinny to be human. They also wore huge, bulbous helmets with fins on the sides. Their wet suits glistened black against the dingy white snow.

They were waiting. They reached out their arms for Mrs. Dash.

Mrs. Dash ran the other way.

She thought she had a chance. She really did. She knew a path through a clearing that would take her to the Herlihys' house. It was just to the left, down the—

Mrs. Dash stumbled into a clearing and came to a halt.

In the center of the clearing, surrounded by black trees with spiky branches, beneath the dark and dirty sky, sat a flying saucer. It had burned away the snow beneath it, so there was one spot of color: the emerald green moss of summer.

Mrs. Dash groaned: a long, sorrowful sound.*

---

* Speaking of mothers and the noises they make, I would like to include a note here about Busby Spence's mother. After his father left to fight in the Pacific Ocean, she hardly talked. In later years, Busby could not remember his mother saying a single thing during the whole Second World War. She was too sad to speak. Of course, she actually did say things, but he could never remember any of them later. He just remembered her standing and washing a lot of dishes, facing away from him. There were only two of them eating now, instead of three, but somehow it seemed like there were many more dishes when his father was away. His mother cooked and washed and cooked and washed.

Busby would try to fill up the silence at the dinner table by telling her about the latest Jasper Dash inventions and adventures. "So, Mom, in *Jasper Dash and His Locomotive Sieve*, there's this machine that makes gravity turn upside down. So things fly. But it's not just like they're flying—they fall *up*, instead of down. It sounds swell, but wouldn't that be awful? Because then there wouldn't be anything to catch you. You'd just fall forever, until there wasn't any air. So there's this one fellow, he's a thug, and he's part of this international ring of jewel thieves, and . . ."

Busby's mother listened, but she didn't say anything. She didn't have any opinion, apparently, about what would happen if gravity was reversed, and instead of things falling down, they, for once, fell ever upward.

And then the aliens closed in on her.

LIMOUSINE FOR THE LORD OF ELECTRICITY

Jasper Dash woke up when shocks of static electricity zapped his hands.

He scrambled into a sitting position. He was lying on the surface of Zeblion III beneath the sculpture of wires.

He swiveled his head from side to side in its clumsy helmet. He saw no one around him. Just the endless range of steep, round mountains with their antennas.

He carefully rose to his feet.

ZAP! Another shock sent him staggering.

Hey! an electrical voice demanded, right by his ear. *Glad to see you're awake.*

Jasper swung around. There was no one there.

"Only cowards bully people without show-ing their faces," said Jasper. "Yellow-livered cowards."

There was a flash of blue. Jasper jumped.

The flash hadn't appeared outside. It was inside his helmet.

"Who are you?"

The electric voice said, *It doesn't matter. Turn around. Start walking toward that bridge.*

Jasper said, "I shall not walk a single step until I am told where we are going."

I've been trapped in those wires for centu-ries. We're going to a city of my people. I'm rid-ing you like a camel.

"I gather you are made of electricity?"

That's right. And I'm sitting in the metal of your space suit. I can give you a shock at any time.

"Very well," said Jasper. "I will walk you to your city. It is over this bridge?"

Over this bridge.

Jasper followed the spark's orders. He asked, "Did your people build these antennas?"

No. We were brought here.

"Who brought you?"

The Dirrillillim.

"Who are the Dirrillillim?"

The inhabitants of this world. They brought us here as prisoners, way back. Through some kind of teleporter machine. They're gone now. I haven't seen a Dirrillill for years.

"So why, mister, aren't you already at the city with the rest of your people?"

I was just on vacation. You know, to get away from it all.

Jasper did not believe him. He walked across a huge brown plain. In the distance, he could see the glitter of more wires. He figured that it was the city of the spark people.

Jasper asked more about the Dirrillillim who had brought the spark person to this world. The spark man didn't answer. Jasper stopped walking. He folded his arms.

ZAP!!!

"Jupiter's moons! All right! I'm walking!"

It seemed like forever as they crossed the plain.*

Finally Jasper said, "I think you weren't on vacation at all."

I was on vacation. I was relaxing. Enjoying nature.

"The only thing more cowardly than bullying is lying."

The spark said, *All right. I was in prison. When the rest of my people moved to their new city, they left me trapped back there, in the ruins of the First Wire City.*

"I'm sure they had a very good reason," said Jasper. "And I am not going to help you escape any prison."

He stopped talking and turned around. "Here I stand," said Jasper Dash. "I will not be a limousine for an electrical jailbird. I am no getaway car."

---

* I hope you're not wondering how Jasper and the intelligent spark understand each other. They are speaking Espace-eranto, the common language of all worlds. I don't really know how to explain the electrical being's knowledge of camels.

ZAP!!! BRRRKKVVVP!!!

Jasper almost fell down this time. It took him a minute to regain his footing. The spark didn't say another word.

Jasper straightened himself up shakily. He heard a dangerous buzzing in his ears. He kept trudging toward the wire city of electricity.

No Air for the Weary

Katie Mulligan and Lily Gefelty were reassembled fifteen hundred light-years from home.

They were in a big booth.

There was no air.

Frantic, holding their breath, they tried to struggle into the space suits Katie had pulled out of Jasper's closet. They were a tangle of arms and legs.

Lily stuck her feet in her suit and then her arm, and then Katie's glove whapped her in the face.

"Sorry!" Katie coughed out quickly, giving up precious air.

Lily's elbow accidentally knocked Katie's skull—"Sorry!" Lily croaked—and Katie's helmet whammed into Lily's shoulder—"Sorry!"—and then they were both hopping on one leg trying to get the boots to fit.

Lily bounced onto Katie's foot.

"Ow!"

"Sorry!"

Their lungs were almost empty. Their eyes were bulging. They forced the helmets onto their heads. They were shaking, fighting with the clasps.

Lily turned around. Her forearm nailed Katie in the back. Katie stumbled and kicked her in the leg. "Sorry!"

"Sorry!"

"Sorry!"

"Sorr—" Lily did not finish the word. She couldn't. She was out of air.

There was no oxygen whatsoever in her lungs. She gagged. She started to see stars. She gripped onto the wall of the teleporter booth. She grabbed at her throat and slid down to her knees. She panicked on the metal floor.

She had been too polite for her own good.

Katie reached over and held her friend's helmet firmly and flipped the locks into place.

Lily heard the hissing of her air hoses. She gulped.

She could breathe.

She drew a big breath. Again and again.

And gratefully, she sighed, "—rry."

* * *

"There's something wrong with this," said Katie, looking around the dead Welcome Home party. "This doesn't feel right to me."

"Jasper was here," said Lily. "Look at all the scuffs in the dust." She ran her suit's fingers over the cardboard hats and the limp balloons.

Katie said, "I don't like it. This party doesn't feel good. And remember, I'm someone who's been at parties with nail-toothed, carnivorous dolls."*

Lily walked over to the drooping WELCOME

---

* Horror Hollow #27: *Sleepover of Doom.*

HOME. She picked up the trailing JASPER off the floor and tried to stick it back up. The tape was too old and dry. "Poor Jasper," she said.

"Something is not right," Katie said again. She walked forward with her hands spread out. "It's—It's—I've got it!"

She rushed over to the table where the cake sat, sunken in its own cracked frosting. She grabbed a lump of it with her space-suited fingers and cried, in wild disgust, *Fruit-and-nut cake! It looks like chocolate, but they made him FRUIT AND NUT!*" She threw the cake blotch down on the ground as if it had burned her. She backed away, scrubbing her hand off on her hip. "His favorite is chocolate with chocolate frosting. What kind of a person . . ." Katie shook her head in shock.

Lily said quietly, "It might not be a person at all."

That made them both fall silent.

"We gotta find him," said Katie. She walked over to the door. "He's out there somewhere."

She yanked the door open.

And suddenly the whole chamber was wailing with sirens and blaring with lights.

Lily and Katie reeled backward as the walls screamed.

SHOCKING!

Jasper Dash and his electrical passenger had reached the Second Wire City. Wires were strung in every direction between pillars of stone. The wires sparkled and tinkled with activity as energy beings zapped through the circuitry and bunched up to see the approach of the strange animal of metal and flesh.

Ugh, said the spark in Jasper's suit. *Now I remember why I was an evil dictator. Look at them all. My former subjects. They're terrible people. All they care about is glitter and sizzle. I really can't stand them.*

Jasper watched the wires sway where the beings crowded.

"You were an evil dictator?" he asked his rider.

The Dirrillillim put me in charge of the rest of my people when we were brought here. I tried to get them all to simmer down. Through executions and frequent groundings.

"But you've learned your lesson after your long imprisonment, and you're ready to return?"

No. I have not learned my lesson. That's why I needed the metal on your suit to carry me between the old First Wire City and this new Second Wire City. My people kicked me out and exiled me long ago. I am going to invade them and rule with hideous might for a million years.

Jasper stopped walking. "I don't believe in any kind of dictatorship."

ZAP!!!

Jasper jumped.

The voice said, *You don't have any choice.*

"No! By gum," said Jasper, "I have never played the patsy for any evil electrical dictator, and I never will!" He stood stock-still, stubborn as a mule, with his legs planted firmly on the alien dirt.

Then the jolts started. *ZAP! ZOT! ZOCK! ZIP! ZWAMP!!!*

Jasper danced and gurgled in agony.

He fell to the ground. His hair stuck up straight. He panted for breath.

He had no choice. Deliver this wicked warlord of wattage to his unsuspecting victims—or die of electric shock.

Volt Face

As Jasper crouched on the ground near the Second Wire City, his microphones began to pick up the faint buzzing of voices from the metal web.

Ah.

Hmm.

Yes.

Glory be.

It's an animal.

Fancy, an animal!

In metal.

Isn't there someone with it?

I think I can see . . . Lovey-dove, isn't that Bzzazzokk the Conquerer?

It is! Bzzazzokk! It's Bzzazzokk!

Jasper crawled toward the Second Wire

City. He croaked out, "Never fear . . . small electrical people . . . I shall not allow Bzzazzokk to corrupt your glorious network! Live in freedom!"

ZZAP! Jasper cringed as Bzzazzokk sent another electrical shock right through him.

But just as Jasper prepared to resist heroically, he heard the voices of the people again, buzzing through the wires.

It's all right, animal! Bring him to us!

Do not resist him.

It has been a long time since we've had an evil dictator.

Bring him hither.

We are bored.

We might as well try an evil dictator again. Perhaps it will be comical or refreshingly diverting.

Jasper lifted his eyebrow. The look was lost on the electrical people. "Jupiter's moons," he said. "Are you sure?"

Step under the wires. Take him to our central node and release him.

Bzzazzokk, flitting around the metal in Jasper's suit, was full of confidence and joy. *See, animal?* crowed the sizzling dictator. *They want me to return! I am greeted in triumph, with shuddering in the wires and great surges of voltage!*

Jasper had learned that aliens often had strange ideas about what made sense, so he wasn't going to ask too many questions. "All right, fellows," he said. "If this is what you really want, I'll drop him off. Where and how?"

The little voices called for him to drop Bzzazzokk off in the city square. It was a knot where all the wires came together.

Jasper leaned down and crawled along through the tangle. The people of the Second Wire City were careful not to jolt him. Still, making it through all the slanting lines and coils without tripping was difficult. The shadows of power lines spidered over his space suit.

After two minutes or so, he was right near the center of the knotted city of electricity.

Thirty or forty tiny voices buzzed,

Welcome, welcome, Bzzazzokk and his noble beast!

Welcome to the Second Wire City!

Rise, animal! Rise and release the warlord Bzzazzokk!

Jasper stood carefully. He raised his gloved finger toward the bunch where all the wires came together.

Bzzazzokk was making a speech. *Citizens of the Second Wire City, you have made me so proud, to be back among you. Many of you I have not seen since you were just a few joules with barely any positive charge. And yet, to receive this hero's welcome, to be able to return for a reign of crazed, despotic terror that shall last a million years, is really more than I expected from—*

Then the full blast of electricity hit.

Jasper involuntarily threw himself backward and bounced on wires like a boxer hurled on the ropes.

Everything was silent.

Slow, small sparks licked up and down the wires.

"Hello?" Jasper whispered.

We're eating, said one of the citizens of the Second Wire City.

There's been a drought. We haven't had any electricity pass this way for months.

No solar winds.

No magnetic storms.

We're hungry.

So we've divided Bzzazzokk up and we're all taking part of his electrical charge.

"You're . . . *eating* him?" Jasper was horrified. "That's . . . That's *awful*! That's *terrible*! You're as bad as *he* is!"

Was.

Ha ha.

"You can't just—cannibalize someone! Even if they're an evil dictator!"

Well, said one of the voices, *in a day or two, we're going to do the same thing to you.*

"To me?!?"

Your body is full of electricity.

Your brain is electric.

Your heart is electric.

Your nerves are electric.

We snack on the body electric.

We'll keep you here until we're hungry again.

"Ha!" said Jasper, pulling out his ray gun. "Keep me here? I would like to see the army that could!"

ZZZZAAAPPPP! They hit him with charge!

He went reeling—bumped into more wires—lit up—rebounded—was flung around like a pinball in a machine that was bursting with thumper bumpers, double scores, triple scores, SLAM TILT!

He fired his ray gun—again—again!

And the wicked little sparks ate up the energy. They cackled. They devoured his battery.

More! More!

They dropped him. He fell, exhausted, to the ground.

All his muscles hurt from jolting. He looked at the twenty feet or so he'd have to crawl and bend himself around and make sure he wasn't close enough for a spark to jump and—

BZZZZT!

They started jolting him again.*

Don't even think about escape! they buzzed. *You're staying here! You're ours!*

You're supper!

Jasper Dash screamed, trapped in a web of fire.

---

* You know who knew a lot about electricity and physics in general? Busby Spence's father. He had a job fixing appliances before the war. When he was sent off to the Pacific, he worked as a radio operator with the Marines. Busby didn't know exactly where his father was. He studied the Pacific on a map—all the island chains. But when letters arrived from Busby's father, everything that might give away a position or a location had been cut out of the letter with scissors. (It would be dangerous if any of that information ever fell into enemy hands.)

Busby and his mother read those letters home again and again. "Dear Flo and Busby," the letters would say. "I miss you something terrible. I can't say where we are or where we're going. I can tell you it has palm trees, that's it. But a whole lot of love, and don't forget your pop!"

It didn't take Busby and his mother very long to read the letters.

They waited for Busby's father to come home.

A Warning from Space

What terrible things happen to people in books. I'm sorry. All I want—all any of us want—is for all these nice people in the stories we read to stop being chased, shot at, electrocuted, taken prisoner, dropped from cliffs, tied to train tracks, locked in caves, gnawed on by griffins, and plunged into the sea.

But we want a good story even more. So just as soon as they settle down, put their feet up, and start to play a slow, quiet game of cards, here we are again—the author and the readers—sneaking up through the bushes to peer in the window, knowing that at any moment some mobsters will bust in, or centipedes will come out of the walls, or the Christmas tree will start whapping people with its branches and ornaments.

Things, for example, are not going great for people in this story. While off in the black-and-purple clouds of the Horsehead Nebula, Jasper Dash was waiting for his electrocution and Katie and Lily were fighting just to take a breath, Jasper's mom—who was also fighting for breath, after her sprint—was surrounded by aliens in the frozen winter forest.

The aliens were tall and gangly and goggly. They had ray guns.

Mrs. Dash said, "I demand to know what you want, gentlemen."

One of the aliens stepped forward. He held up his ray gun. He said in a growly voice, "Are you Jasper Dash?"

"No," said Mrs. Dash. "Jasper is my son. And right now, he's a very naughty boy."

"We have come for Jasper Dash."

"Well, boys, you're out of luck, because my son has gone gallivanting off to the region of the Horsehead Nebula."

The lead alien rocked backward. "The Horsehead Nebula? Then he has already perfected the teleportation machine?"

"You're right he has," said Mrs. Dash. "And when he gets back, he is going to be grounded for a good long time. Those trees'll be green again before that boy gets his shrink-ray privileges back. Why do you want him? Who are you?"

"We have come from the planet of Krilm."

"I haven't had the pleasure," said Mrs. Dash. "Anyway, you'll never catch my Jasper! He's far, far away."

"We are not trying to catch Jasper Dash. We are trying to warn him."

"Warn him?" repeated Mrs. Dash.

The alien explained, "He has walked into a trap. And because he used that teleporter, the whole of the Earth is in peril."

THE SECRETS OF THE DIRRILLILLIM

The aliens invited Mrs. Dash into their flying saucer for a hologram picture show. "It will explain many things."

"Why, that's very kind of you," said Mrs. Dash. "Although it is a little peculiar to receive an invitation to attend a party in my own yard."

They walked up a ramp into the spaceship. Inside, everything was sleek and cool and silver and white. The aliens—who were called the Garxx of Planet Krilm—stood around the outside of the room and pointed at the center.

Suddenly stars appeared in the air. It was a hologram image in 3-D. And as the leader of the Garxx spoke, other images appeared before them.

"Long ago," said the leader of the Garxx, "when your race and ours were young, there was a very old race of creatures called the Dirrillillim. They were a violent and evil race. They came from the planet you call Zeblion III. For generations, the Dirrillillim had flown between stars in spaceships like this, which go at two or three times the speed of light." Suddenly a fleet of gloppy, weird spaceships were hanging in front of Dolores Dash's eyes.

"You made this picture show especially for my son, didn't you?" Mrs. Dash realized. There were tears in her voice. "It was for him to watch. . . . I am so sorry that he was not here."

The aliens shuffled nervously. "We've showed it a few other times to people," admitted one of the Garxx of Krilm.

Another one said, "Each time, we fix the music and stuff to make it better."

"I see," said Mrs. Dash. "And do you show a picture of one of these . . . What are they called?"

"The Dirrillillim. When there's only one, it is called a Dirrillill."

"Very fine. Do I see one?"

"We have never seen the Dirrillillim. We have no pictures."

"They are a mystery, then," said Mrs. Dash.

"Indeed. We know this history only from other races we have met. I shall continue. They tell the tale that the Dirrillillim spread far through the stars in their spaceships. But then the Dirrillillim invented the teleporter. An incredible machine. It would take them instantaneously across the galaxy. The problem was, they could not teleport just anywhere. There had to be both a sending machine and a receiving machine."

Mrs. Dash gasped as she saw a booth that looked very much like the one in Jasper's room. A dotted line was drawn between it and a similar booth that hung near a far star in the diagram.

"Using their spaceships to deliver teleporters across the huge distances between stars, the

Dirrillillim spread their empire across one arm of the galaxy." A map appeared, showing an arm of the spinning Milky Way covered with little lines and dots. Then bursts of light began bubbling up inside the Dirrillillim Empire.

"Then they began to war among themselves. Whole stars were blown up. They were a powerful race. They attacked one another mercilessly. There was a giant blast, larger than any blast the galaxy had seen since the beginning of time. Several huge solar systems were destroyed. This is how the Horsehead Nebula was formed.

"After this war, there were only a few Dirrillillim left. They were trapped on their home planet, Zeblion III. They needed new teleporters on other planets if they were ever going to expand their empire again. And so they began a great project.

"The few remaining Dirrillillim realized that the quickest way for them to get teleporters built on planets they wanted to invade was to *get*

people on those planets to build them themselves.
But the problem was, on many of those planets, there was no one smart enough to build a teleporter. And so this is what they did, Mother of Dash: They *sent signals into space—highly concentrated beams of information from their planet in the region of the Horsehead Nebula.* These signals told how to create hyperintelligent members of the species on each planet. But hidden away in these plans was a secret: After many years of study and learning, these hyperintelligent children on hundreds of different worlds would each receive another signal . . . and in a dream, they would figure out how to build a particular kind of teleporter machine. And they would know to create a link with the Horsehead Nebula. And once this link was formed, then *the Dirrillillim could use their teleporters to invade.* That is the story, Mother of Dash! Your boy has built one of these machines and has traveled to the region of the Horsehead Nebula—where he shall meet the Dirrillillim and shall be

taken captive and questioned! Then hundreds of the remaining Dirrillillim, with their powerful weapons and their ruthless self-congratulation, will invade Earth!"

The pictures faded.

The alien asked, "Do you have any questions?"

Turning to the leader, Mrs. Dash demanded, "So who," she asked, "are you?"

"As we have said, we are the Garxx of Planet Krilm. We are one of several races that intercepted the beams sent out many years ago. We have been trying to follow the beams to each planet so we can find the children the Dirrillillim created. We try to warn them not to build the teleporter. We recently discovered that such a communication was sent to Jasper Dash."

"And how many of these children have you warned?"

The aliens were a little uneasy.

"None," said the leader. "We have always gotten there too late."

"Well, sir, you're a little late again, apparently. My son headed off into the region of the Horsehead Nebula just last night."

"That is unfortunate."

"So what now? How do we save my boy? Do you propose to fly there in this ship?"

The head Garxx said, "This ship travels at three times the speed of light."

This sounds very fast, but in fact, Mrs. Dash knew it was not nearly fast enough. The nebula was fifteen hundred light-years away. That means a ship going exactly the speed of light would take fifteen hundred years to get there, and a ship going three times the speed of light would still take *five hundred years* to get there.

By that time, they would all be dead.

"I see. So what do we do?"

The head Garxx crossed his arms. "We had hoped to have Jasper Dash explain to us the secret of building the teleporter. But instead, let us go inspect the one he built—and perhaps we may learn its secrets."

"And then?"

The Garxx looked at one another. "Then perhaps we can use his teleporter—to invade the Dirrillillim before they can invade you."*

---

* Sometimes Busby Spence's friend Harmon complained about science fiction. "This is what I mean," he would say, pointing at a chapter like this one. "This story is crazy."

"Makes sense to me," said Busby Spence.

"Want to do something else?" said Harmon, tossing down his Jasper Dash book.

"Gee, okay," said Busby Spence. "What are the other guys doing?"

"Today?"

"Yeah."

"What's today?"

"Sunday."

"They're stealing scrap. From the high school's scrap heap. So they can put it on the junior high's scrap heap. And we can have more scrap for the war. I think we win a prize. A letter from the governor or something."

Both boys thought about this. Stealing scrap didn't sound very fun.

"You know what?" said Harmon. "Forget I ever said anything. Let's read."

They sat in the second tree house and listened to the rustling of the leaves and the burping of contented raccoons. Across town, boys lugged rusted bumpers and old tires across vacant lots.

Grasshoppers fled before them through the tall, dry grass.

RECIPE FOR DISASTER

Jasper Dash sat surrounded by a web of metal wires, waiting for his electro-execution.

"I do not think this is very fair," he told the sparks who watched around him.

No, it won't be fair, they replied. *But it will be tasty.*

Jasper pouted, but secretly, his brain was working at full power to try to figure a way out of this fix. He could tell there was no way to talk these hungry sparks into letting him go. They were too vain and selfish. Somehow, he had to think of a way to escape.

He looked up through the metal strands at the violet heavens. The scene would have been beautiful, if jagged, lightning-like death hadn't been threatening to end the afternoon with a loud, crispy jolt.

Then Jasper had an idea.

He called out, "I wonder whether you fellows would at least let me eat my last meal."

Go ahead, said one of the sparks. *We'll cook it for you.*

There was a sizzle of laughter around him.

"That won't be necessary, fellows," said Jasper, rummaging around in his backpack.

His food wasn't fancy, but it would be fine for the occasion.* He brought out another tube

---

* Jasper Dash, Boy Technonaut, did not need anything fancy to eat. He had made it through the final years of the Great Depression, when there wasn't very much food, and the Second World War, when food was rationed by the government so there was enough for the troops fighting overseas.

Busby Spence, longtime reader of Jasper Dash novels, knew that rationing was important so that soldiers like his father could eat—but still, he didn't like it. Almost immediately when America entered the war, sugar was rationed. Soon there was no candy left in the store near Busby Spence's house, and there would not be candy for sale there again for years. After a few months, a lot of other things went on the rationed list too: a lot of meats, even butter . . . almost everything that made food good. He stared at his plate as everything got more and more tasteless and pale. He was often still hungry after dinner.

of sandwich, a few squirts of french fries, his saltshaker, and some water.

With dignity, he drank a sandwich.

He shook a few dehydrated water pills into a metal saucepan and added water. They made even more water.

There was a lot of buzzing in the lines around him.

Don't mind us, said the citizens of the Second Wire City. *We're just deciding who gets the left lobe of your brain and who gets the right lobe.*

Jasper nodded. He went about his cookery.

He prized off the lid of the saltshaker and poured all the salt into the saucepan of water.

At that point, Busby Spence convinced his mother to buy Jasper Dash's Victory Spread, a dark, sticky, weird-tasting thing you put on bread. No one really knew what was in it. The label said, in big, cheerful letters,

DON'T ASK! JUST OPEN YOUR JAWS WIDE!
EACH JAR OF VICTORY SPREAD IS MADE WITH
100% VICTORY!

This was not strictly true. Unless "victory" usually means suet, ground carrot, grass clippings, and whipped pork fat.

He stirred it around with the finger of his space suit.

Will you think really hard when we're eating your brain waves? the sparks asked. *It might make them juicier.*

Jasper finished stirring the salt into the water. He tapped his finger on the rim of the saucepan. Then he stood up.

"Swell," he said. "Now that I've eaten, I will thank all you fellows if you let me go on my way."

Fat chance! said the sparks. *Nothing doing!*

You're our community supper! Everyone's coming!

"You should let me go," said Jasper. "Otherwise, there will be a big disaster."

You want a big disaster? said the sparks. *Maybe it's time for you to say your good-byes.*

"I'll say my good-byes," said Jasper with dignity. He looked around at the live wires and bid them, "Good-bye."

The sparks surged. They were about to jump the half inch through the air to kill Jasper!

They revved up.

Blue shot along the wires.

Thousands of volts zapped toward the Boy Technonaut—

And at that instant, he tossed the pan of water onto the big knot of wires. Salt water went everywhere!

There was a loud, bright *KRAK! BVVVVVT! KRAK! POW!*

There was a universal sizzle!

Jasper Dash had shorted out the Second Wire City.

Then everything around him was silent.

Off in distant parts of the city, there was the screaming of energy beings who'd just figured out what had happened.

Jasper made his escape. He rolled and jumped and tumbled through the net of wires. Now no one tried to electrocute him as he fled from the web.

He landed on his feet outside the Second Wire City. He backed away before they recovered.

"I mixed salt and water," he shouted back to them. "Salt and water together make an excellent conductor of electricity. So I overloaded the wires near your town square. Next time, don't try to eat other living, talking beings! Because honesty and hospitality always triumph over cannibalism!"

He turned on his heel and marched away from the energy people of the Second Wire City.

For a while, he heard their little electrical voices thrumming behind him: *Come back! Come back!*

We just want to give you a massage!

We'll recharge your ray gun for you!

We'll light up the whole city for you! We know disco!

But he didn't listen.

Because after a few steps, he'd looked over toward the antenna where he'd first arrived on the planet.

And he saw that someone was headed right toward it. Someone in a flying car, shooting over the mountains.

Someone, finally, had come to meet him.*

---

* On the other hand, Busby Spence, Jasper Dash's biggest fan, waited for months and months—and even years—to throw a welcome home party. It was going to be for his father, who was off in the Pacific. Busby Spence and his mother got a note from Busby's dad saying that he was going to be sent home for a couple of weeks before he was sent into action on a different island.

They prepared everything for his arrival. They cleaned the sofa and beat all the rugs to get the dust out of them. Busby raked the leaves so the lawn would look good.

Then, two days before Busby's father was supposed to arrive, he called, saying he wouldn't be coming. His unit was sending him off to a radio training session instead. He told them he would not be making it back to the East Coast.

Busby's mother slammed down the phone without saying good-bye. Then she immediately started crying and wanted to call him back. She didn't know the number, though. He was at a pay phone.

A few days later a package arrived from Busby's dad. Inside it was a metal statue of a god in some robes, and a note that said, "To my two favorite people. Here's a god of good luck I found where we were just fighting. He has to apologize in person for me not coming, since I can't be there to say sorry myself. And Flo, I *am* so sorry. You know what coming home meant to me. I think about you two all the time. You're all the world to me. Signed with love. From your pop, kid—and Flo, from your loving husband."

Busby's mother was happy to get the letter. She put the little statue of the god on the windowsill at the top of the stairs. She smiled at it and patted its head whenever she walked by.

Busby sized up the statue after brushing his teeth. In a Jasper Dash book, any worthwhile statue of a god sent from a distant tropical island would be cursed, and it would come alive at night and try to kill him and his mom. Or at least people would *think* it was cursed, until Jasper Dash discovered that the statue was actually a radio receiver that was sending messages to the enemy.

Busby Spence picked up the statue and shook it.

This stupid statue was no secret radio. He couldn't use it to talk to anyone. No one could use it to say anything to him. No secret messages were coming from anywhere.

Busby's mother left the statue there at the top of the stairs. It looked down on all their comings and goings.

Busby used it to play ringtoss with the lid from a canning jar.

This Time, with Flare

Jasper rushed across the green, glassy hills, waving his arms and leaping.

Here he had come fifteen hundred light-years—and he might miss the person who was coming to meet him!

He jumped up and down, almost yelping with the effort.

But he was a tiny dot on a huge landscape. The flying car slid through valleys toward the distant antenna.

Jasper started running toward it as fast as he could.

He knew there was no way he would make it there in time.

"By the Greater Magellanic Cloud!" he brayed.

He grabbed his ray gun out of its holster. He held it straight up and fired several bolts of light into the sky. They were not bright: The electrical people had sapped the gun's energy.

The aircar was still headed away from him.

Desperately, he fired a final few shots—killing the batteries.

He watched across the huge gulf as the aircar quivered in the sky. He longed for it to turn around and come to him. It was time for his party. Time for his cake. Time to find out what his whole life was about.

. . . And the aircar turned. Someone had seen him. The flying ship zipped across the chasms and canyons and made its way straight for him.

Jasper didn't know how to contain his happiness. He hopped up and down and waved again.

It might be his father in that aircar!

It settled down near him, kicking up a fine green dust.

A door on the side slid open.

Jasper Dash happily stuck his ray gun back in its holster.*

He waited to see who would come out of the dark portal.

But what came out was not exactly a "who."

---

* Busby Spence wished he had a ray gun like Jasper Dash, Boy Technonaut's. He wanted to be able to point it at battalions of tanks or enemy ships and, with a huge blue bolt of anger, make them all disappear. When he went to the movies and they played a newsreel before the show, he watched the scenes of battle—the eruptions in the water; the white wisps of tracer bullets in the air; the dull gray landscapes flowing beneath planes, blossoming with blasts; the dark antitank guns lifting up and rearing back—and Busby imagined himself there with his ray cannon, squinting his eyes cruelly and making the whole terrifying Nazi Wehrmacht disappear in a burst of light.

Of course, when he thought about it, he realized Jasper Dash's ray gun ran out of batteries too frequently. For this reason, he decided he preferred Captain Galactic's sonic blaster, even though Captain Galactic wore dumb boots.

Once, when he and his mother were sitting in the movie theater, waiting for a new episode of *Captain Galactic*, the newsreel showed some of the fighting in the Pacific. There was a picture of a tropical island. The tide was coming in, and the bodies of dead American soldiers were floating facedown in the water.

Busby Spence's mother got up and yanked Busby up the aisle and out of the theater. They missed the movie.

That was the episode of *Captain Galactic* where they finally reached the castle of Drong, Slayer of Worlds. Busby Spence never forgave his mother for making him miss it.

It was a huge lump of human parts: legs, arms, men's eyes, women's eyes, many mouths (some with mustaches), and ears like shelf fungi on trees.

It paused on the top step of the aircar, looking down at Jasper Dash. Various eyes looked him up and down, from his space-suited head to his magnetic boots. It blinked at him.

Then it bumbled its way down to the ground.

It said, "You are, perhaps, from Earth?"

"I'm Jasper Dash, Boy Technonaut." Jasper stuck his hand out. "It's a pleasure to meet you, sir."

The creature looked around. "Ah! Which hand would you like to shake? It's a very special

day, Jasper Dash, and I want you to have anything your heart desires."

Jasper looked at the selection: hairy arms and muscly arms and weak arms and trick arms. "Gosh, I think I'll choose that one, sir!" he said.

He shook hands with a good, middle-of-the-road arm.

"Jasper Dash! If it isn't Jasper Dash! It's a pleasure to meet you finally!" said the creature. "I am the Dirrillill."

"Was it you who set up that swell party for me?"

"It certainly was, Jasper. That was me! I baked that cake with my own hands. These three."

"Gee, it sure was nice of you to bake a cake to welcome me to the region of the Horsehead Nebula!"

"We try to welcome everyone to the region of the Horsehead Nebula."

"And you must be the one who sent that beam of information about me to Earth?"

The Dirrillill thought about this for a second. Then a mouth said, "Of course! Of course! Yes, it was a while ago, back when there were a few more Dirrillillim around. But I am sure that I remember sending the beam of information about you to the planet Earth. Yes, absolutely! How could it slip my mind? It was, now that I think of it, the happiest day of my life!" He sighed. "It has been very difficult here. All the final few Dirrillillim, my friends and colleagues—they have all died in the last fifty years—tragic, very tragic. I am now the only Dirrillill left. It is very lonely. I have not been able to follow up on all my interstellar friendships the way I hoped to. So I am delighted that you are here! We shall have a grand time!"

"You'll show me the sights?"

"All of them. Of course, of course! Right after we go back to your home planet, and you can show me the sights there! Aren't you excited? Hop in the flying car, Jasper Dash."

The Dirrillill could not have seemed nicer. But, see, because you and I have read other chapters, we know that this staggering blob of bits and bobs was *two-faced*, and not just because he had at least two faces. We know to listen for a dangerous, growling edge to everything the Dirrillill said. We know what peril Jasper put himself in by jumping happily into the creature's flying jalopy.

But Jasper wasn't really thinking. He was too happy to put two and two together. He figured, *Never mind what those electrical chaps said. This Dirrillill creature is a swell sort of fellow, and not the type to imprison anyone without a very good reason!*

So Jasper hopped into the Dirrillill's flying car. The last of the Dirrillillim swung a hand around, and a ring of symbols and controls appeared in the air as if on an invisible, floating screen. With some of his hands, he fiddled with the glowing controls. With the other hands, he made gestures while he talked.

He said, "I hope you don't mind if I ask to see Earth before I show you around here. I have always wanted to see the planet Earth. That's where you come from, isn't it? Grand. What do you say we just pop on over right now? It would give me great pleasure to have you show me the sights. The capital cities, for example, where there are the largest number of humans all gathered together. We'll go now, lickety-split. Sound grand?"

"Why, it does sound grand! You're almost like a . . . an uncle to me or something, aren't you?"

The Dirrillill thought about this. "Well . . . Yes, certainly! Yes, Jasper Dash, I'm just like an uncle! Think of me as an uncle! In fact, think of me as all your relatives, mixed together! Rolled into one! Aunts, uncles, cousins, perhaps even a father or two."

"A father? Really?" Jasper couldn't believe it. He drew breath so quickly it was almost like a gasp or a sob.

Some of the Dirrillill's eyes turned and looked carefully at Jasper. The Dirrillill read Jasper like a book. Then one of its mouths said, "Sure. Exactly, ha ha. A father."

Jasper could hardly stand still, he was so excited. He bobbed up and down on his tiptoes. "I can't wait for you to meet my mom!"

"She pretty?"

"You bet!"

"Boy, this is the best day ever!" the last of the Dirrillillim exclaimed, clapping with several pairs of hands.

Jasper said, "By the rings of Saturn, we're going to have a swell time!"

The Dirrillill pushed a floating button. They lifted off and hovered with the mountains around them.

As it turned out, they were not going to have a swell time.

Just as the Dirrillill was about to fly them toward the Earth antenna, Jasper mentioned, "I met some awful electrical fellows a little while ago. They were frightfully zappy."

"Them? I didn't know they were still around."

"Do you know, they told me that you and your people imprisoned them. I knew it couldn't be true. I'm sure that you have an excellent explanation."

There was a long pause. The Dirrillill didn't say anything.

So Jasper hinted, "Which you'll tell me right now."

Some of the Dirrillill's mouths smiled uneasily and said things like, "Yes," "Ah," "Oh!" "Um," and "Well, it's like this . . ."

Jasper smiled. "Yes?"

One of the mouths was just about to say something when another one bellowed, "I don't wish to change the subject, but Jasper Dash, did you arrive alone? All by, shall we say, your onesies?"

"I did, sir."

"See, that's a strange thing. I got a second alarm signal, as if someone else had followed you, ha ha. Wouldn't that be lovely? If we had more company? More friends, more fun?" The Dirrillill inspected him. "Do you know anyone who might have followed you?"

Jasper thought about his mom, back on Earth, and his friends Lily and Katie. He was a little embarrassed he'd left them behind, especially when everything was going so well with his . . . gosh, with his father, you could say. His father the Dirrillill.

"No," said Jasper. "No one else was supposed to follow me."

"You've got company at your party," said

the Dirrillill. "We're going to Earth's teleportation station anyway. Let's see what we find."

With a quick motion of his hand on the floating controls, he swooped the car in a circle and flashed across the plains.

Something That Begins with "Danger"

Lily and Katie sat side by side on one wing of the antenna. They looked out over the weird landscape. They dangled their legs and tapped their feet together.

"Nowhere," said Katie. They had found some of Jasper's footprints, but after a while, the ground got too hard. They couldn't follow his path anymore. They had given up. Katie said, "I can't believe he left without us. I could kill him right now. Who runs away from your friends to a dangerous other planet?"

They were getting worried.

Lily wondered how much air they had left in their tanks.

Then suddenly, Katie grabbed her arm.

"What is it?"

Katie babbled, "I see something. I spy with my little eye, something that begins with . . . What actually is that? *M*? *F*? *C*? *R*? *Q*?"

Something skimmed along toward them through the purple sky.

It was a flying car.

The two of them scrambled down to meet it.

It slowly sank down and came to rest.

Lily and Katie were a little worried when the door opened. They didn't know what they'd see.

But there was Jasper, smiling a big smile inside his space helmet and holding out his arms.

"Jasper!" yelped Katie with happiness.

And then they saw behind him, in the shadows, a hideous tumble of arms and eyes and legs and noses.

Lily blew her hair up out of her eyes to get a better look.

And the eyes stared right back at her, full of suspicion and rage.

DEATH RAYS FOR EVERYONE!

"Lily! Katie!" exclaimed Jasper. "By the glittering eye of Thoth, it's good to see you again! Look! This is the Dirrillill. He is something that is kind of like my father!"

The Dirrillill stepped heavily out of the flying car and held out many hands to shake. Too many. It was like meeting ten people at once.

As Katie and Lily shook some of the hands and introduced themselves shyly, Jasper said, "Why, isn't this swell? Fellows, I'm fit to burst!"

The Dirrillill said, "Grand to meet you."

Katie said to Jasper, "You just went off and left us! We're your best friends! We felt hurt, and then we got attacked by a thing with goggle eyes!"

Jasper looked embarrassed for a second. Then confused. Then he said, "Well . . . but . . . I've just met . . . well, Mr. Dirrillill, is it all right with you if I call you my . . . my father-like thing?"

The Dirrillill laughed heartily. "Of course!" he said, and slapped Jasper on the back several times from several different directions.

Now that Lily had been introduced to the Dirrillill, she felt bad for thinking that he had looking angry and evil. Sometimes it's difficult to feel good about someone who has more than two hundred teeth. Lily made a decision: She was going to like this Dirrillill for Jasper's sake, no matter how strange he might look.

The Dirrillill bustled inside and over to the teleporter booth. "So—what do you all say we pop back to your home planet for a little bitty look-see?" He touched the controls while his mouths blabbered backward, "I really do love going to new places and meeting new people."

"No!" said Katie. "There's a monster there. Or at least, there was an hour ago."

The Dirrillill swiveled. "A monster?" he said. "Do tell."

Katie and Lily told the story about the thing that had invaded Jasper's home and chased Jasper's mother off into the woods.

"Mother?!?" said Jasper. "We have to go right now and save her!"

Lily opened the door to the booth.

Katie looked at the Dirrillill and said, "I'm not sure that, uh, *everyone* is going to fit in Jasper's booth on the other side." She raised her eyebrows. "I think that even if we go one at a time, *everyone* might not fit in alone. *Everyone* is a little big for booths."

The Dirrillill said, "I take it that you are speaking of me and my magnificent plurality. Jasper Dash, will I fit in your receiving booth?"

Jasper looked uncomfortable. He shook his head.

"I see. I see." A look of anger passed quickly over the Dirrillill's parts of faces—like a crowd at a baseball stadium doing The Wave—but then it was gone. "That's a disappointment. I would like to go to Earth and save your mother. I tell you what: What about let's stop by the Final Fortress of the Dirrillillim—my own home sweet home—and I'll show you around, pick up some more equipment I may need on Earth, and then we'll send you back to your home planet so you can enlarge your teleporter booth and then your—ha ha!—your chubby pal the last Dirrillill can zap back over with you and see your super planet. Sound grand?"

"What about my mother?"

The mouths said: "Your mother . . ." "Yes . . ." "Your mother . . ." And finally one piped up, "Please, tell me, Lilah and Caitlin, when did you teleport through? Did you say an hour ago?"

"Lily and Katie," said Katie. "Yeah. It was like an hour and fifteen minutes ago."

"Well! Ah! There we are!" The many mouths smiled. "Time moves differently here. We're on a different world. If you fled from

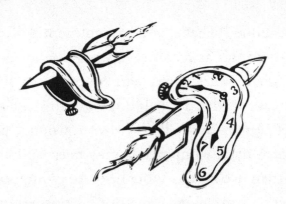

some beastie, is that what you say? Yes, so you fled from this fiend an hour ago in the time of this planet. Well, that is only a few minutes on Earth. Maybe a few seconds! If you go back now, he'll still be there, crouched by the booth and waiting to snap you up like a rubbidith with too many phylooges."

Katie said, "What's a rubbidith? What's phylooges?"

"A local animal. Private joke. Too complicated to explain. But look, my other mouths get it." The other mouths were grinning toothily. "Look, children, come with me. We'll go over the mountains to the Final Fortress of

the Dirrillillim, my home. We'll get the necessary parts and equipment to enlarge the booth
on Earth and we'll get, oh deedly dee, a whole
stack of weapons. Then we'll come back, send
the three of you through to polish off whatever
space monster is moving in slow motion, chasing your excellent mother. Then, young Jasper
Dash, you will enlarge your teleporter booth for
me. Sound grand?"

"Yes! You can give Lily and Katie some electric rays too, so they can fight this monster?"

"Of course! Of course!" The many smiles
smiled. They smiled very wide. They said,
"Yes! It will be death rays all round!"

You and I have read other chapters in which
Mrs. Dash heard about the secret evil of the
Dirrillillim, so his promise to deliver death rays
for everyone probably does not sound very
reassuring to us. But remember, Lily, Jasper,
and Katie hadn't heard anything the Garxx
of Krilm had said in their holographic moving picture show. So the three kids thought

they were going to zip back to Earth shortly and stop a space monster in its tracks, saving Jasper's mother and solving the mystery of the alien invader.

So they said things like, "Great!" and "Let's go!" and (Lily) "Can we just set the death rays to stun?"

And they all bundled into the Dirrillill's flying car without a fight and let him drive them farther and farther away from the interstellar gateway back home.

LIGHTS OUT FOR THE DIRRILLILLIM

Katie did not like the Dirrillill. She did not trust him. She was watching him carefully.

He steered the flying car through the green glass mountains by twiddling his fingers in the air, touching glowing controls that appeared and hovered around him.

"La dee dee, la dee dah," he said.

The whole time, he was watching Katie back, watching Lily, and very carefully watching Jasper.

Jasper's brows were tugged down, and his mouth was serious.

Katie asked, "How're you doing, Jasper?"

"I'm just dandy, Katie, but I won't rest easy until we've saved my mother."

"Here we are," sang one of the Dirrillill's mouths, "on an adventure together! What fun! What fun!"

Katie did not think that "fun" was a word the Dirrillill should be using. She could tell the Dirrillill was lying about something. Katie was a world expert on many-armed monsters, because of her experience as the heroine of the Horror Hollow books. So she knew this monster was secretly evil. It bugged her. She watched him swoop them over vast, hairy plains. She said, "Wow, sir, you're really handy with this flying car. Reeeeeally handy. Handy, handy, handy."

Jasper and Lily looked up, a little shocked that Katie was making jokes about all the Dirrillill's hands. The Dirrillill stared straight at her—at least a few regions of it did.

She stared right back into several of the eyes, as if to say, *Listen, buster: If you hurt my friend Jasper, you're going to be in trouble.*

And the eyes looked back at her, saying

things like, *Don't meddle with me*, and *You are powerless here in my domain*, and *Ha ha!* and *Mm-hm?* and of course the classic, *My dear, you cannot possibly imagine my evil plans.*

In ten minutes they were on the other side of the mountains, and they had come to a giant city. It was dead. There were looping ramps and huge, bulgy apartment buildings. There were hovering fountains, which now just dribbled a little water. They hung above dried-up gardens.

"Once the capital city of a great Dirrillillim empire," said the Dirrillill. "Now they're all gone but me."

Jasper looked out in wonder at the wild buildings and crashed airships. "What happened?"

"None of us got along very well with each other."

Now the three kids started to notice huge, clean holes in a lot of the buildings. They couldn't tell whether the holes were a popular architectural detail or the scars of disintegration rays.

"Of course, you want to see the sights!" the Dirrillill's many mouths exclaimed. "Over there's Mount Yondo. Once volcanic. Now full of secret caves."—"That's the old Palace of Justice there. Unfortunately, no longer staffed."—"Crashed over there is our Guvnalillalla Stadium. Where we played guvnalillalla."—"And down that avenue, the big building with all the fins is the opera house. As you can imagine, opera was a great art with the Dirrillillim. I mean, we have so many mouths, each one of us can sing as a whole chorus. You should have *seen* the costumes, back in the day. Unfortunately, with only one of us left, opera is a dead art. I have recordings of some of the great performances of our golden age. Lussminniffine Ssabriss as Queen Toast, walking through her empty castle, wailing for her lost children. Six thousand years later, it still brings a tear to the eye." He pointed to one of his eyes. "This one."

The kids were amazed by everything they saw. But at the same time, there was something sad about this empty and desolate city. There were no lights to be seen. All the windows were dark. Most reflected the red, angry sky. The planet felt huge and dead. The lights would never go on again.*

---

* During World War II, there was a song called, "When the Lights Go On Again All Over the World." It was too slow and sappy for Busby Spence. (The numbers he liked on the radio were "Let's Put the Axe to the Axis," "Six Jerks in a Jeep," and the one where Spike Jones farted in Adolf Hitler's face.)

But "When the Lights Go On Again" was one of Busby's mother's favorites. While Busby lay on the couch, reading Jasper Dash stories, the song would croon out of the radio, recalling men risking their lives in fleets halfway across the world, soldiers setting up camp on unimaginable isles, boys lying with rifles on battlefields in French farmyards while bombs shook the ground around them.

It had been two years since Busby had seen his father.

Busby Spence lifted up his head.

"When the lights go on again
All over the world,
And the ships can sail again

"What happened to everyone else?" Lily asked, aghast.

"It is tragic," said the Dirrillill. "Very tragic. Oh, the savagery of the Dirrillillim, the need to conquer and rule. We fought so long and so hard with ourselves that all of us died. Except me, of course, ha ha."

"Gee," said Jasper, "I'm sure glad you were safe! How did you avoid getting killed when there was all that mass destruction?"

"Oh, lo, lo-dee-lo-lo," hummed the Dirrillill.

All over the world,
Then rain or snow is all
That may fall
From the skies up above.
A kiss won't mean good-bye,
But hello to love."

Busby Spence saw that his mother was slow-dancing alone in the kitchen, with her face down, as if it were pressed into someone's shoulder. A wet plate was still in her hand.

And the radio sang:

"When the lights go on again
All over the world
And the boys are home again
All over the world . . ."

"I don't recall exactly. I was safe behind those walls." He pointed at a huge, glowing, spiraling metal castle covered with antennas. "The Final Fortress of the Dirrillillim," he said. "My place."

DINNER WITH THE DIRRILLILL

The Dirrillill switched off the shimmering force field around the castle. He flew the car into a parking space on the roof. The force field snapped back on, a glowing carpet of energy that was draped over the whole fortress. There were several other old, ruined ships sitting on the roof.

The hulking Dirrillill heaved himself toward the door and clambered down. "Let's go in and get you some ray guns. Jasper, I'll draw up a quick plan for how you can create a larger teleportation booth. It shouldn't take you long. We'll be on Earth in the twitch of a mufftagreeb."

Jasper said, "How long is that?"

Some shoulders shrugged. One mouth said, "We'll be there in a couple of hours," but another one corrected, "I mean, a couple of hours in *our time*, ha ha." A third mouth explained, "Only a few bare little minutes will have passed on Earth. Sorry for the old force field. Since I am the last of the Dirrillillim, everything is kind of run-down around here."

The old force field around the building was droopy and heavy like a big tarp. It hung all over everything. They had to lift it up and hold it over their heads while they walked across the roof toward a door. When they got to the door, which slid aside, the Dirrillill very politely propped the force field up with several elbows so they all could get inside.

The inside of the tower was a weird mixture of ramps and open spaces and bulbs and globes. The kids followed as the creature waddled through huge hangars of alien weaponry.

Jasper said, "Sir—sir, I just am so happy to meet you. And, well, I hope it's okay if I say that I'm very proud to be going on this adventure with you."

Lily and Katie exchanged a glance. They could both hear that Jasper was trying to talk in a lower, more manly voice than normal. He was almost shivering with excitement.

Shyly, the Boy Technonaut admitted, "I've always dreamed of, um, meeting you, sir, and . . . well . . . defeating invaders. Together."

"Sure, sure," said the Dirrillill carelessly. "It's grand. Grand! So, when we get to Earth, what sights will you show me?"

"Gee," said Jasper, "I don't know where to start. First, after we save her, you'll have to meet my mother. Her name is Dolores."

"I shall be delighted." (In fact, Katie thought that the Dirrillill looked kind of bored on most of his face-parts—like what Jasper said didn't really matter.)

Jasper continued, "Then maybe we'll all go out for ice cream at Persible Dairy. Then we could go on a world tour. We could fly to the Eiffel Tower in France. Or to Ayers Rock, in Australia. It's a big rock, and—"

"A big rock," said the Dirrillill, swaying along on his several legs. "Fascinating, fascinating. I am really looking forward to this visit. Ice cream is . . . ?"

As they passed through a hall of missiles and bombs, Jasper tried to explain about ice cream. He talked about the cow and the milk and the udders.

The Dirrillill listened and said, "So, to welcome me to your world, you offer me a fluid that drips from the bottom side of an animal, but cold."

"Why, when you say it like that, it doesn't sound so good, sir, but let me tell you, ice cream is a swell treat."

"Lovely."

"Just one bite, and it's not just ice cream you can taste: It's also summer, and vacation, and green, growing things, and sitting on the porch, licking your spoon, and the bees."

"Stinging insects?"

"I'm trying to paint a picture, sir."

"Green . . . On your world, it is the color of growth?"

"Yes, sir," said Jasper. "It's beautiful. All the trees and the grass are green. It's the color of chlorophyll."

"I don't know her, but she sounds adorable. Here, green is the color of decay. For the Dirril-lillim, green means death and putrefaction."

They had come to a large kitchen. There were weird appliances all over. The kids had no idea how any of them actually produced food.

The creature said, "First, why not a little bite to eat, hm? Chompy chompy?"

Lily, who was getting concerned, said, "Do we have time? Shouldn't we be—"

"Don't worry about it, Lilah. Always time for a square meal, or, in my case, several octagonal ones." The Dirrillill opened a drawer and pawed through a bunch of pamphlets while another couple of hands fiddled with gadgets. "I have some take-out menus here. I don't cook much myself." He shoved the menus at the kids. "Take your pick. The cuisine of any world in this arm of the galaxy. From back in the days when this world was full of people from all over our empire."

Katie said suspiciously, "Why are there restaurants? I thought you were the only Dirrillill."

"I am. I keep the restaurants in business. I have a lot of mouths to feed."

"Who runs the restaurants?"

"Machines, nowadays," answered one mouth, and another suggested Dludge food, and a third recommended, "Don't try the Skraxflange menu. The Skraxflanges were a silicon-based life-form, and they mainly ate dry clay with a gravel garnish. Very embarrassing when you order a dish at their restaurant and you literally get a dish. Ceramic. Crunchy but tasteless."—"Ah. Here's an Earth menu. There you go."

Katie looked over the entrées. "Ankylosaurus stew?"

"Their idea of Earth cuisine may be a little out of date."

"Diplodocus fritters?"

"You're fifteen hundred light-years from home. You take what you can get."

"I guess I'll get the buffalo allosaurus fingers."

"Sure. Appetizer portion or meal?"

"The salad."

Lily said she just wanted the butter-fried ferns.

"That's it?" said the Dirrillill.

"I've been thinking of becoming a vegetarian anyway," Lily said. "And I guess I don't want to eat anything that's already extinct."

Jasper said he wanted the fritters. The Dirrillill called in their orders. He himself was getting several different meals for different mouths.

With other hands, he had done a little sketch of what Jasper would have to do to expand the teleportation booth back on Earth. "You see?" the Dirrillill said. "I can give you the parts. You'll have to put them together on the other side. You think you can do that for your old pal the last Dirrillill?"

Jasper looked over the plans. Lily could see he was bursting with pride. The Boy Technonaut was obviously thrilled that the Dirrillill was asking him for help. "Sure, sir," he said. "I'd be honored."

"Honored. That's swell, ha ha." Another mouth said, "It's a pleasure," and another one said, "Let's get working after dinner. The sooner you can fix your teleporter up, the sooner you and I and your mother and your little friends here will be relaxing, dreaming of stinging insects, and eating a big, delicious vat of cold cream."

"Ice cream."

"You can understand my error. Let me go up and gather the spare parts."—"Hit this button when the food arrives. It will let the food robot through the force field. Got it, kids?"

He was about to walk out when Jasper said to him: "Sir? . . . Mr. Dirrillill? Will you . . . will you stay on Earth for a while? With my mom and me? We have room in our house of the future. And that's where the teleporter is. You know, why, you can go back and forth from this planet as often as you want." The hope in Jasper's voice was raw and awful.

"Aren't you a nice guy to invite me?" The mouths smiled sweetly. "Oh, don't worry. I'll be spending a lot of time on Earth." With that, he gave an evil grin—but it was only with one mouth, very low down on his body, and facing the other direction. No one could see it.

But Katie's eyes still scrunched up with distrust. She glared at the Dirrillill. He lumbered away, humming to himself with many voices.

Katie turned around, muttering to Lily, "Wonder if he wants a hand with anything. . . . Don't worry—we can just keep an eye on things down here. . . ."

Lily gave her a warning look and said to Jasper, "Are you, um, having a good time, Jasper?"

Jasper grinned. "Just about the best day ever, chums!" He gazed happily out the window at the tiger-striped sky. "Who would've thought that later today I'd be off to save my mother with a death ray supplied by my own father-like thing."

Katie cleared her throat loudly. She tapped her finger angrily on the counter. "There is something fishy."

"What's fishy?" asked Lily.

"I don't know. But everything on this planet is fishier than a stingray in a grouper in a killer whale. I don't trust that Dirrillill!"

Jasper said, "Ever since you've met him, Katie, you've been very rude."

"Because I'm sure he's evil. Where are all the other last Dirrillillim? Nowhere! He got rid of them all! He's the winner of their war! He killed them and won a dead planet."

Jasper's cheeks turned red. "I will thank you not to say things like that about my father. Like. Creature. Thing. And I might mention that the killer whale is not a fish. It is a mammal."

"Katie," said Lily, "you haven't given the

Dirrillill a chance. Just because he has so many teeth."

"*So many teeth!*"

Jasper crossed his arms. "You are being terrible, Katie. I would like you to apologize to the Dirrillill."

"He's planning to take over the Earth! You can tell!"

"That's balderdash."

"How do you know he's nice?" Katie argued. "You don't know him. You haven't been on this planet much longer than us!"

"Six hours longer. And I know my aliens."

Katie rolled her eyes.

"Katie," said Jasper seriously, "I no longer feel at home on the Earth. And it was always my friends who made me feel at home. You. So now that I have the chance to have a family—a real, honest-to-gosh family—I wish you wouldn't ruin it."

"What about your mom? You have your mom! You don't need some monster!"

"He is not a monster!" Jasper was almost in tears.

They would have kept arguing, except that the doorbell rang.

A little screen appeared in midair. It showed the foot of the tower. A robotic vehicle with several bags of take-out food waited to be let in through the force field. The force field shimmered and buzzed.

"Delivery," said the robot.

Jasper and Katie both went for the button and paused over it, giving each other a dirty look. Then they both pressed it at the same time.

The force field lifted up. There was a click and a whir. Down seventy levels, a little door opened, and the robot placed the food in a little elevator, then crawled away. The force field dropped.

A second later Lily saw a door on the counter open. Up popped several stapled paper bags with different restaurants' logos on them.

Katie opened the bag from the Blue Marble Bistro ("Earth to Go!") and lifted out the kids' Jurassic meals.

Jasper crossed his arms and said to Lily, "You might tell Katie that I am not going to start eating until our host comes back. Because I am polite."

"Oh," Lily pleaded. "Please don't do that thing where you don't talk to each—"

"Jasper may be interested to know that I was actually just getting out the food to see whose was whose."

"Katie might wish to hear that I'm getting out the silverware."

"Lily, could you tell Jasper that he'll need a bunch of extra sets of knives and forks for his evil, all-devouring new best friend?"

"Lily, could you remind Katie that the Dirrillill just very kindly bought us dinner?"

"Lily, could you tell Jasper that I can't find any napkins, so we're going to have to use paper towels?"

"Lily, could you—"

"Ah—eh!" said Katie. "Look what the Dirrillill's eating. . . ."

The others glanced over at the containers she'd popped open. Some of the meals were curled and hairy, baked in syrup. Lily was not entirely sure that when they were alive, they wouldn't have been able to talk.

Lily backed away from the take-out containers.

"What?" said Jasper uncomfortably. "It's just food."

Katie was looking in horror at Dirrillill's feast. And then, weirdly, she said, "Jasper . . .

Did you say you'd been on the planet for six hours before you met us?"

"Lily, you can tell Katie that yes, I—"

"Just answer the question, Jas," said Katie. "Because if that's true, then—"

The door slid open and the Dirrillill waddled in on his several legs, pushing a cart of machines, spare parts, and ray guns in front of him.

"Dinner, dinner, dinny-poo, ha ha!" the Dirrillill exclaimed, rubbing some of his hands together. "Aren't you thoughtful to set the table?" The alien hobbled over and squatted near the plates. He picked up knives and forks and began to serve himself his hideous meal. He encouraged the kids, "Dig in!"

Jasper held up Katie's Styrofoam box of dinner and said, "Lily, you might inform Katie that apparently allosauruses have two fingers. And that they are served with a dipping sauce."

No one else spoke.

The Dirrillill asked, "Why the long faces?"

Katie said, "We could ask you the same question."

"I'm sorry, sir," Jasper said to the Dirrillill. "She doesn't mean to be rude."

"Yes, I do," said Katie. "I mean to be very rude. Because what time did you leave Earth, Jasper?"

He shrugged. "It was about three in the morning."

Katie said, "Well, at seven o'clock in the morning—four hours later—your mom discovered you were missing. And she freaked out and picked Lily and me up at seven thirty. And we teleported here at about eight o'clock. And then Lily and me looked around for you and waited for an hour."

The Dirrillill pointed at Katie's food and sang out, "Someone's letting her dino diner dinner get cold!"

"SO," Katie insisted, "that's about six hours. Six hours on this planet, six hours on Earth! In other words, *there is no difference between how*

time goes here and at home. In other words, WE
ARE SITTING HERE MESSING AROUND
WITH TAKE-OUT FOOD WHILE YOUR
MOM IS FIGHTING SOME MONSTER
BACK ON EARTH!"

She shoved the Styrofoam box away from
her, and it toppled off the table. She pointed at
the Dirrillill. "He tricked us! He doesn't care
about your mom! He's just trying to get you to
go back and fix up the teleporter so he can go
through and invade! You see? That space monster fooled us all!"

"Oh, ah, ha ha," said the Dirrillill. He dabbed
at a mouth with a paper towel. He stepped
toward the three kids. "Please," he said. "Call
me Uncle Dirrillill."

His hands grabbed knives and forks, and,
swinging them, he growled and screamed and
laughed all at once, lunging at the children.

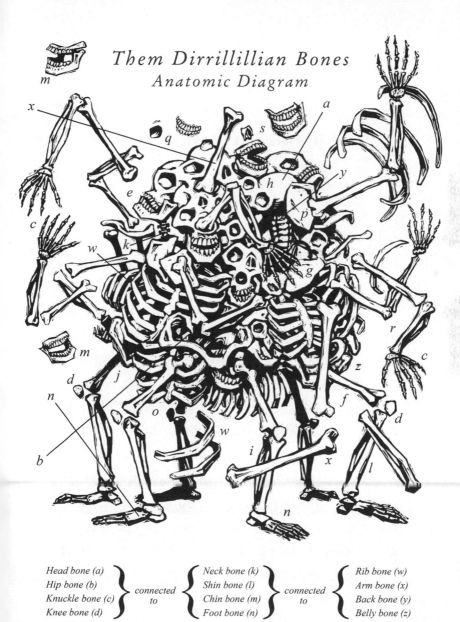

Them Dirrillillian Bones
Anatomic Diagram

Head bone (a)		Neck bone (k)		Rib bone (w)
Hip bone (b)	} *connected*	Shin bone (l)	} *connected*	Arm bone (x)
Knuckle bone (c)	*to*	Chin bone (m)	*to*	Back bone (y)
Knee bone (d)		Foot bone (n)		Belly bone (z)

THE DIRRILLILL DISHES IT OUT

Lily cowered in fear.

The Dirrillill swung the knives and forks through the air menacingly. "Look here, Jasper Dash, one way or another, I'm going to need you to go back to the Earth and enlarge that teleporter booth so that it's large enough for me and my weapons."

Jasper said, "I will do no such thing. Is Katie right? What are you planning? What's going on?"

"'What's going on' will be all your cities, one after another, being scrubbed off the map by my disintegrator ray until the people of Earth submit to me, ha ha. I alone, the last of my kind, shall rule a new empire! Earth shall be the first bauble on my new imperial charm bracelet!" The Dirrillill swished his cutlery through the air—about to dice young Dash like some delicious dish.

"I won't do it!"

Then the Dirrillill darted toward Katie and swiped his knives toward her. She yelped and jumped back. The creature said to Jasper, "Which of your friends would you like me to kill first? That's what will happen if you don't go back to Earth and set up the teleporter for me, ha ha."

"I thought you were my family!" Jasper complained, tears coming to his eyes. "But you're just like the rest of the aliens I meet! Boasting about invasion!"

"Too true! Too true!" said the Dirrillillim— and he dove toward Katie, slashing.

Katie was not helpless, even when attacked by someone with many more arms and legs than her. She held up a chair with enough seats for three butts. With a clang, the knives hit the chair!

The kids ran for the kitchen door.

"Come on, Jas!" yelled Katie.

"I'll hold him off!" said Jasper, pulling out his ray gun.

Lily and Katie heard laser bolts being fired. They ran up ramps. They ran through rooms with bulbs and rooms with tubes.

They were in an echoing armory where missiles and bombs hung in brackets.

"Jasper's not behind us!" said Lily. "He's still back there!"

They hesitated.

Jasper—all alone—was engaged in combat with the creature he called his father.

HOME SWEET HOME

Of course, Jasper's ray gun hadn't done him much good. It had basically been sucked dry by the electrical people, so it was completely out of juice.

But Jasper had also studied hand-to-hand combat, and he sprang into action.

The Dirrillill stabbed at him with forks and knives!

Jasper leaped!

He kicked!

He hit the Dirrillill squarely in some of the faces!

The Dirrillill aimed a swift left and three rights at Jasper's head. The Boy Technonaut dodged just in time, and each punch flew—*swish!—swish!—swish!—SWASH!*—right past his skull.

Jasper punched, but hands repelled him.

He kicked—and connected—but the Dirrillill had grabbed his leg.

Jasper hopped on one leg, fists wheeling.

The Dirrillill threw him down—then, with a spare hand, grabbed a gadget, aimed, and fired.

Suddenly Jasper was frozen. He tried to push himself up, but his arms wouldn't move. He tried to turn his head, but his neck wouldn't move. He could see everything, but he was helpless.

The Dirrillill picked up the paralyzed Boy Technonaut. "Very sorry, son," said the Dirrillill. "I know this isn't what you were expecting here in the Horsehead Nebula. But don't worry. Very soon—very soon—your Earth will be part of my empire. So in a way, ha ha, you'll be home, even when you're imprisoned here forever."*

---

* One day Busby Spence got home from school and found his mother sitting in the living room with both her hands and a letter pressed between her knees. It was a letter from the US government about his dad. She gave it to Busby to read.

> Dear Mrs. Spence:
>
> On behalf of the United States Armed Services, we regret to inform you that your husband, Lt. Henry Spence, has been wounded in action and has been removed to a hospital facility. He will receive a medical discharge upon the removal of his casts and a period of psychological evaluation.

From what Busby understood, it meant that his father wasn't going to be in the Marines anymore. He was going to get an honorable discharge. Busby was so happy he yelped. He couldn't understand why his mother wasn't more thrilled.

After years of Busby never even seeing his father, his dad was finally coming home.

NINE AND FIFTEEN ZEROS

Katie and Lily stood in the weird shadows of the armory, listening.

"What do you think happened to Jasper?" whispered Katie.

Lily's eyes were wide. She had no idea what to do.

Katie walked a few steps back toward the door they'd just come through.

Then they heard the slapping of many feet, running together like a Roman legion in an old gladiator movie.

"A whole crowd," whispered Katie. "Of one."

It was the Dirrillill thundering toward them.

They darted toward a ramp. They remembered the way up to the roof.

They ran through the strange architecture of the Final Fortress of the Dirrillillim. Lily looked back.

She saw the reflection of the many-faced creature pursuing them across surfaces of glass. It doubled the hands, the mouths, the eyes, the arms that grasped.

"Girls!" called out one of the Dirrillill's mouths, while others said, "Ladies!" "My dears!"—"We won't hurt you!"—"We simply want to hold you hostage until we need to kill you!"

Katie and Lily scampered out onto the roof. They were far above the surface of the planet. Heaving the droopy force field over their heads, they made their way between old flying cars resting on cinder blocks.

The Dirrillill called out to them. "Let's go! Back inside, girls!"

Stooped over, they crept toward one of the cars that looked like it might still work. They hid. They flattened themselves against the side. They hunkered down.

Above them, the old force field twitched and yanked as the Dirrillill raced around the roof, looking for them.

Lily could tell she was starting to breathe too much and too quickly. She was gasping with terror. Sometimes Lily wished her friends wanted to spend a normal weekend sitting around the house, watching stuff on the computer. She closed her eyes and wished herself magically to be sitting on the wall-to-wall carpeting in her living room, with the three of them making Rice Krispies treats and drawing interlocking lizards on their math book covers. As she heard the alien's footsteps approaching, her panicked brain could picture perfectly every detail of every single piece of furniture in that living room: the scrapes on the coffee table, the pattern of the sofa, the cushions on the chairs, the bricks of the fireplace, the little black freckles where the rug had melted when sparks flew past the fire screen. . . . It was all in front of her eyes.

But it was fifteen hundred light-years away.

The footsteps were coming up right beside the flying car.

The monster was right near her, but Lily couldn't even think about it—no!—so she just squinched her eyes closed, hysterically calculating that if the Horsehead Nebula is fifteen hundred light-years from Earth and one light-year is about six trillion miles, then . . .

FIFTEEN HUNDRED LIGHT-YEARS = NINE QUADRILLION MILES!!!
9,000,000,000,000,000 MILES!

Lily shivered. *She was NINE AND FIFTEEN ZEROS MILES from her mother and her—*

She opened her eyes and saw about twelve knees.

"Aha!" said the Dirrillill. "Dooby dooby dooby doo."

The girls pushed away from him as fast as they could.

But there was nowhere else to go. They were on the edge of the roof. Lily looked down. It was about a hundred stories to the ground. Instant death if they fell.

The Dirrillill stalked toward them. Several arms held the canopy of force field up so he could get a clear shot at them. He had a gun.

"I froze your friend because I need him. I'm not sure I need you." He clicked a knob on the gun. "So let's try disintegration, shall we?"

He did not make the mistake some bad guys make: talking a lot before firing. Though he had many mouths, he just didn't have that much to say anymore.

So he just shot the girls there and then.

What Goes Up

. . . Except that Katie had yanked down a fold of force field just in time between them and the monster. So the shots crackled and were absorbed.

Lily stumbled on the edge of the roof. Just under her heel was a drop to the death. Her breath was too fast. Her head was reeling.

The Dirrillill cleared some throats. He said, "All right."

Lily couldn't believe that this was it. . . . About to meet her end! Nine quadrillion miles from home!

"Maybe I can't hit you behind that force field," said the Dirrillill.

"Nope," said Katie smugly. "You can't."

"But I can destroy the roof you're standing on, ha ha."

The Dirrillill fired near their feet.

BLAM!

The corner of the roof disintegrated. The girls screamed as they fell off the top of the fortress.

Silence.

The lip of the fortress was gone.

The girls were gone with it.

Where they had stood a second before, there was nothing but purple sky and violet tiger stripes of cloud.*

---

* You lie on the ground by the lake and watch the clouds drift over like a slow, grazing air raid.

Once, Busby Spence lay five feet from where you are now. There was more grass there then. He read there for a long time, trying not to think about things too much.

Unfortunately, as you know, this yard was always full of ants.

The Dirrillill smiled and smiled and smiled. All over him, he was grins.

Having destroyed Katie and Lily, he wobbled back inside to start working on Jasper Dash.

THE ANGRIEST PLACE MAT
IN THE GALAXY

The Dirrillill lumbered back into the kitchen. Jasper Dash was still frozen in place, unable to move, unable to yell out to Katie and Lily.

The creature smiled. "I have destroyed your little friends. Lulu and Kaylie. I blew up the ground they were standing on. They fell to their death. A pity they didn't have a hand or two more to grab a railing. But then, Kaylie never did like my extra hands. Remember her, my boy? When she was alive, ha ha?"

Jasper Dash's head swam in horror. He wanted to fight—to scream—to *hurt* the Dirrillill, like he'd never wanted to hurt anything. But he couldn't move.

The Dirrillill thumped over to Jasper and

picked him up, grunting. He dropped the frozen Boy Technonaut on the kitchen counter. He straightened out Jasper's arms and legs. The joints creaked like cheap hinges.

"You must learn to submit," the creature of many eyes and mouths demanded. "You will serve me. You will go back to Earth and enlarge that teleporter booth so I can go through with my gear. And Earth will be the first world to be captured by the new Dirrillill Empire. *My* new Dirrillill Empire."

Jasper tried to budge an inch. He tried to shift one arm, then the other. He couldn't even grunt with effort.

"Do you see," said the Dirrillill, "you are nothing more than furniture to me, ha ha. I may use you like I do a chair or a table."

The alien trundled over and picked up some of the food. He brought it back to Jasper and laid it out on top of Jasper's belly, face, and knees, as if the Boy Technonaut was just a bumpy place mat.

The Dirrillill said, "Now, isn't this a quaint way to dine? Off a human being?"

The alien picked up a forkful of some hideous, furry, gravied beast. It dripped its sauce on the Boy Technonaut's faceplate.

As one mouth chewed the morsel, another said to Jasper, "You're not important to me at all. I can always do without anyone."

He ate his feast on Jasper's face.

It was many courses. Hands shoved different dangling globs into waiting mouths. The Dirrillill, being somewhat rude, leaned his elbows on the table while he ate. That meant six elbows, all of them pinning Jasper down. Jasper couldn't shift to make himself more comfortable. He couldn't roll away. He had to just sit there with Styrofoam plates on his belly and two sodas perched on his shanks—and these were supersize sodas.

When the Dirrillill was done with his disgusting degustation, he announced, "Now for the pièce de résistance, ha ha. Maybe I will eat you yourself. Yes?" He reached down with two of his hands and began to gently pull at Jasper's helmet. "For that, I am afraid," said the Dirrillill, "I will have to remove your oxygen mask. Sorry: The atmosphere on my planet will not agree with you. You will choke and die. But luckily, you are frozen, so I will not hear a miserable peep out of you."

The alien started to unclip Jasper's air hose.

DOLORES DASH TAKES A STAND

Mrs. Dash sat in a chair at Jasper's desk. She watched the Garxx of Krilm crawl all over the teleporter booth, making whispery noises to one another. They were trying to figure out how it worked.

"Can I get you boys anything?" Mrs. Dash asked. "Root beers? Finger sandwiches?"

The Garxx of Krilm were not interested in snacks.

Mrs. Dash was sick of waiting. She folded her hands together and squeezed them very tight. She opened Jasper's desk drawer and pushed around the erasers with her thumb.

Mrs. Dash felt sick with guilt. She should have stopped him from going somehow.

She thought about what a terrible mother she was. Now, as a result, her son was off looking for a father among a race of cruel alien invaders. And his friends were probably trapped with him.

She said, in a voice that was almost angry, "Can't we just go through the teleporter as it is—right now—and rescue the children? The girls must be there too. You frightened them away, appearing with your . . . with your big, big heads. Can't we just go save the children from these Dirrillillim—and then you boys can figure out all the secrets of intergalactic travel afterward?"

One of the Garxx of Krilm stood up and said, "Please, patience, Mother of Dash. The Dirrillillim will be waiting on the other side with weapons and trickery."

"Well, how is *all this*"—Mrs. Dash gestured furiously at their tinkering—"going to help?"

But the Garxx of Krilm did not answer her

questions. They turned back to the booth and kept inspecting it, speaking their hissy, whispering language.

"Do you understand?" said Mrs. Dash. "I tried to protect my son, and I failed, and now he's more than a thousand light-years away. I tried to protect my son's friends, and I failed again, and now *they* are also, presumably, more than a thousand light-years away. I do not want to sit here while you *tinker*. Is this understood?"

The aliens did not speak to her.

But she couldn't wait any longer to act.

She stood up from her son's desk chair. She announced to the Garxx, "I am going."

They turned to her in surprise. They said, "You shouldn't."

They said, "The Dirrillillim will be waiting for you."

They warned her, "You will suffer the same fate as your son."

And Mrs. Dash proclaimed, "That's exactly

what I want." She told the Garxx, "I'm off to get my oxygen gear."

She was back in ten minutes, dressed in an old fifties space suit, from back when women's space suits were pink and had little skirts.

"This is a mistake, Mother of Dash."

She declared, "Don't worry about me. I've been hiding in this house for years. But I am a scientist, and like all scientists, I am trained to deflect heat rays, escape space dragons, and safely land a lifeboat capsule on the cooler parts of the sun. Now. Off to Zeblion III. Any of you coming with me?"

The Garxx gawked.

They said, somewhat nervously, "Well, why don't we stay here?"

"We'll guard the teleporter booth."

"It would be awful if someone tried to pop through."

"So we'll just stay put."

"Hmm," said Mrs. Dash. "I see, boys. Scared."

"Scared? Scared? The Garxx of Krilm? We laugh at fear!"

Mrs. Dash said tartly, "Well, if over your laughter, you could clear away from the booth, I'd be grateful to you."

She stepped into the teleporter. It was pretty self-explanatory. It was already set for Zeblion III. There was a big lever to pull. Mrs. Dash saluted the Garxx of Krilm and pulled the lever.

The Garxx watched her flicker and disappear.

The teleporter was empty.

One of the Garxx said, "The Mother of Dash is gone."

"She will not be back," said another.

"The Dirrillillim will kill her."

The Garxx all looked at one another. Then one said, "Good. Now let us get back to examining this remarkable teleporter machine. That's what we came for."

"That's why we followed those Dirrillillian message beams to Earth."

"That's why we sought out Jasper Dash."

"In an hour we will have figured out the secrets of teleportation."

"Then we can start our crime spree."

"We can use teleporters like this to appear in intergalactic banks."

"And in grand mansions in the space stations that circle Saturn."

"Our treasure chests will be filled with precious metals forged in the Big Bang."

"Our saucer will be detailed in gold."

"We will have warehouses full of diamonds crushed into being under alien atmospheres and stupendous gravities."

"Our pockets will be stuffed with precious laruvium, the most unstable element in the universe."

"Yes."

"Indeed."

"That will be great."

They nodded their huge, finned helmets.

This was, in fact, the plan of the Garxx of

Krilm, who were wanted crooks all over the galaxy. They had intercepted the beams sent across space not to help other worlds, but to find out the secret of teleportation so they could carry out their nefarious plans. And they were only about an hour from reaching their goal.

And while they talked about it, Mrs. Dash was being flung across the universe—fifteen hundred light-years—nine quadrillion miles— far, far from Earth, her island home.*

---

* When Busby Spence's father got home from the war, discharged, Busby and his mother were all dressed up. They went to the train station to meet him. Busby had to wear a bow tie. They had plans to go out to a big dinner at a restaurant and eat all the things they normally couldn't eat because of rationing.

Busby's father got off the train at three forty-five p.m. He was still wearing his uniform. Busby's mother went and hugged her husband. Busby's father did not smile or laugh.

Busby felt shy. He hadn't seen his father for two years. Busby's father didn't look very good. He looked pale and his face was thick from medication. One of his hands was red and covered with scars.

His father just said, "Hi, Buzz," as if he were coming home from work and there was nothing special about the day. He asked Busby's mother, "Do you have the car?" He picked up his duffel bag.

That was it.

Busby was confused. He wanted a big bear hug, like fathers gave their sons in movies. He wanted his dad to shout, "How you been, chief?" or, "Missed you so much, old sport!"

His father was already walking away, down the platform, carrying his duffel bag.

When they got home, Busby's father didn't ask to hear what had been happening. He didn't tell any stories about the things he'd seen blown up. He stood for a while in each room of the house. He walked down to the lake, trudging through the snow, and he looked across the ice.

When he came back inside, Busby's mother said, "We planned a real special evening. We're going to Dana's Cuddleside for dinner."

Busby's father just shook his head. He said, "I got to sleep for a while. Don't wake me up."

He went upstairs, and they could hear him crying.

Busby and his mother just sat on either side of the table, staring at each other, pretending not to hear.

Busby's father didn't come down that night. They canceled their plans at Dana's Cuddleside.

Busby went to bed and read about Jasper Dash hunting Nazis on the ocean floor, deep down where everything is blind or glows.

LATE FOR DINNER

Just as the Dirrillill was about to ease Jasper's helmet off his head and bite into the boy's skull, there was a loud beeping sound.

The Dirrillill rushed over to a panel and touched it.

"Someone else has arrived from your tele-porter!" he said. "Your delightful mother, per-haps." He chuckled to himself. "I've got to go check the screens and see who showed up for your welcome home party without RSVP'ing."

Jasper lay there helplessly. There were still Big Gulp drinks on his knees.

The Dirrillill said, "Don't worry. I'm not going to eat you. Nothing doing, ha ha. I would never eat you until I'm done using you. I am just trying to be convincing. You will want to help me fix that teleporter on Earth. There are lots of ways to convince you. I've already killed your two best friends. And now I suspect your dear momsy is here with us on Zeblion III. I won't destroy her—if you agree to help me conquer Earth. She'll make an excellent hostage. So: I'll pop up to my control room to check if it's her. You think carefully about who you want to save: your mother or your planet. Which do you love better, my son? Hmm?"

Then he left the room, humming happily, while Jasper lay on the counter, still unable to move.

A FROZEN ENTRÉE
THINKS ABOUT THE STARS

Jasper Dash, frozen, stared out the window. He could move nothing. Fifteen minutes passed. He couldn't blink. His eyes were burning. He stared at the stars. They could barely be seen past the glare of violet dust.

Back on Earth, the stars seemed friendly. It didn't matter that they were far away. The stars seemed comfortable, and the Milky Way, spread across the sky, seemed like home. He knew facts about them. He had stood on his porch with his mother on thousands of nights, and they had spotted comets and dying suns and newborn worlds.

Now he was looking up at the same galaxy, but nothing seemed friendly. The stars, after all, were not the smiling, long-lashed pointy fellows stitched onto his baby blankets years ago. They weren't singing anyone songs. They were just chemical reactions, something burning, energy yoked. Everything was cold. There was more emptiness in the universe than stuff. Worlds were just tiny clots of dying warmth in between those infinitely chilly spaces where there was nothing at all.

Jasper's mother had taught him about the stars and about the dinosaurs and about everything else. That's why Earth and all its sciences seemed comfortable, like home, even if the sun seared and the dinosaurs snapped and tore.

The words of awful Uncle Dirrillill rang in his ears: *Your mother or your planet. Which do you love better, my son?*

Jasper struggled. He gagged. He couldn't move—but he had to.

Several rooms above, the Dirrillill was looking at a floating image. There was Jasper's party with its sad streamers and collapsed cake. There was Jasper's mother, standing in the doorway, looking out onto the bleak surface of Zeblion III.

She had tried to tape up the "Welcome Home, Jasper Dash" banner, too. As the Dirrillill watched, grinning with many mouths, the dusty tape gave way again, and the greeting slumped to the floor.

Meanwhile, down in the kitchen, Jasper heard a loud beep. He tried to turn his head to see what it was, but of course he could not.

Just out of the corner of his eye—where he

could barely make anything out—just there, the screen connected with the food hatch clicked on. Someone was down there, standing by the door.

Two forms. Blurry, because he couldn't move his eyes to look directly at them.

But they were smudges that seemed a lot like Katie and Lily.

SOME SCIENTIFIC THINGS HAPPEN

"Katie and Lily?!?" you might say.

You might say, "I thought they fell to their deaths!"

Not exactly.

They were blown off the roof by the blast, yes. And yes, they fell—and they saw the rocky ground shooting up toward them—and screamed—and spread out their arms—and tumbled—

And felt the old, heavy force field scraping against them—

And grabbed onto it.

They grabbed onto the force field and clung, like mice digging their claws into a shower curtain.

Oh, come on. It's totally scientific. This

kind of thing happens with force fields all the time. If you can't pierce them, then you must be able to grab onto big bunches of them like they're an old canvas tarp thrown over someone's motorboat for the winter.

It's PHYSICS.

They didn't move. They just hung there.

They waited for the Dirrillill to leave the roof.

Up above, he stood near the crumbled edge of the landing pad, smiling to himself lots of times.

Satisfied, he went inside to eat dinner off Jasper Dash.

"Okay, okay," said Katie, panting. "We've got to . . . let ourselves . . . down . . . slowly. . . ."

She loosened her grip and slid down several feet.

Lily was still dangling up above her. "I can't let go! I can't make myself! I can't!"

"Just take a deep breath," said Katie. She listened for a second. Then she said, "Okay. Take fewer deep breaths. Lily? Fewer. Lily! No! If you keep taking that many deep breaths, you're totally going to faint."

Lily unclenched her hands a little from the fabric of electricity.*

She scraped downward.

Katie slid down after her.

They slid and skidded past windows and cannons, clutching the force field.

Thump!

They were both on the rocky ground.

"Now what?" muttered Katie.

"We have to save Jasper," said Lily. "Who knows what's going to happen to him?"

Katie nodded. "How are we going to get to him?"

Lily said, "We've got to get back in."

"You've got to be kidding."

"Look," said Lily. "There's the hatch the food went in. Maybe we can get in through there."

---

* Remember: IT'S SCIENTIFIC. DON'T ASK QUESTIONS.

"I'm bigger than food."

Katie was not actually bigger than many of the things the Dirrillill often ate. I say that in a menacing kind of way.

There was not much room between the force field and the side of the building. They had to scrunch themselves up and slide along the wall.

But they were right near the hatch.

As they approached it, they heard a loud beep. The hatch had seen them.

JASPER TAKES A NOSEDIVE

Out of the corner of his frozen eye, Jasper could barely see the two lumps examining the food hatch. He struggled to move. He tried to make a sound, but he couldn't even unclench his teeth.

He heard the voices of his friends. "I don't know," said Lily. "Nothing seems to open the hatch."

"You've tried pulling?" said Katie. "Maybe the Dillirrillirrillum pulls."

"Yeah, and I've tried pushing and sliding. You can probably only work the hatch from that button on the counter. If only there was some way to press it . . ."

Jasper strained. He was on the counter right next to the button. If he could only roll

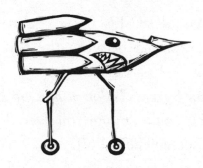

a little bit . . . before the Dirrillill got back . . . he could press it. . . . He could get them in to save him. . . .

With all his might, he tried to heave.

And there was a little motion. He actually wobbled.

Katie said, "Well, we're going to have to look someplace else. Come on."

Jasper heaved again. He rocked a little.

Lily said, "All right. Maybe there's another door."

No! Jasper thought at them. He rocked desperately. The Big Gulp drinks toppled to the side and spilled. Cheap soda pop crawled across the countertop.

He could see his friends starting to walk away, smooshed between the force field and the wall.

Argh! By the Teflon mines of Neptune! he swore. He couldn't quite roll over. . . .

The screen clicked off.

He wanted to sob, but he couldn't move his face.

The screen clicked on again. "Did you hear a sound?" Lily said. "It sounded like someone thumping over a loudspeaker."

Slowly, deliberately, Jasper began trying to roll over again, tensing his dead arm, his half-thawed leg, and his wooden belly.

"I didn't hear anything," said Katie, shrugging. "Let's go look around the other side."

Jasper could hear his own ragged breathing through his clenched teeth. He tried not to panic. He tried to budge . . . wobbling his hips and shoulders as if he were doing disco. . . .

"Maybe we'll have more luck over there," said Lily miserably. She began to walk away.

Jasper grunted.

Almost there . . .

(Katie had started to climb over a rock.)

Almost there . . .

(Lily had climbed over the rock and was outlined against the purple sky.)

Yes . . . Almost there . . .

With a final *whap!* Jasper flipped and hit the button!

Hurrah!

And then he kept on rolling . . . *No!* . . . off the counter and onto the floor. Ouch. He could not move as he lay there. He was behind the counter, smooshed next to the refrigerator.

But he heard the voices on the monitor. "The little door!" Lily cried out. "It just opened!"

Jasper panted with relief.

He heard someone clamber into the food elevator.

There was a hum as it rose.

And then he heard a distant noise: many footsteps.

The Dirrillill was coming down to demand a decision: Earth or Mom.

Jasper's father-like-thing was coming back.*

---

* After Busby Spence's father got home, he spent months walking from one chair to another chair and then sitting down again. He did not talk much with Busby or with Mrs. Spence. He didn't seem to listen to much they said. He often cleared his throat.

Years later, Busby remembered his father always sitting slumped to one side during the last year of the war. Either his left shoulder was higher than his right, or his right shoulder was higher than his left. He sat unmoving, as if he had been paralyzed by some alien freeze ray while smoking a cigarette. His face was pale and large and he breathed smoke and watched people without speaking. He did not seem interested in anything Busby did—in baseball or in reading or in chasing away the raccoons from the tree house. Busby's father didn't seem very interested in anything.

Mr. Spence went out sometimes to try to get work, but they lived too far from cities and there were not many jobs at that point in the war. After a day of hunting for work, he would come home and walk slowly through the rooms, not saying much.

Busby and his mother learned to sort of ignore Busby's father. They just went about their business. Busby set the table, and his mother made the supper, and then Mr. Spence arrived and sat down and ate silently, except when he cleared his throat. After supper he got up and went into a different room.

At first Busby tried talking to him sometimes. Busby's father shrugged and said nothing. Busby felt then like he himself was the one who had been hit with the freeze ray and his face and even his heart had stopped working. His blood slowed down. He stayed standing right there, not moving—while his father walked away slowly.

A Side of Mashed Dash

The little door on the counter slid open, and Katie and Lily uncurled themselves. They were in the kitchen, kneeling in puddles of no-name cola. Faintly, they heard many feet heading their way.

"The Dirrillill! He's coming!" whispered Lily.

"Where's Jas?"

"I don't know! We've got to hide!"

They lowered themselves off the counter.

Jasper was still mashed next to the fridge. He struggled desperately to make a noise.

Lily said, "I hope he's okay."

Jasper's face turned red as he tried to scream. The footsteps were getting closer. There was no time to dally. Katie waved to Lily, and the two of them stepped out of the room and into a hallway. They flattened themselves there and listened.

The Dirrillill stumped into the kitchen, several mouths whistling in harmony.

Eyes flicked back and forth, up and down.

"Where, where, where has the Dash kid gone?" said the Dirrillill. He thumped around the counter. "Aha! You fell behind the counter like an old corn chip." The Dirrillill went over and got a broom from a closet. With several of his arms, he maneuvered it behind the counter and rattled and bumped and scraped Jasper until the paralyzed Boy Technonaut thumped out onto the kitchen floor. "Voilà!" said the Dirrillill. "Now I'm going to unfreeze you so you can speak." The Dirrillill shot a faint ray at Jasper's head.

Jasper gasped with relief. He squinched his eyes shut. He opened them again. He worked his cheeks.

"All right, all right," said the Dirrillill. "It is indeed your dear mother who's come to visit, I believe. So: Have you made your mind up? Will you help me invade the Earth?"

Jasper declared, "By Jove, *never*! Never in a thousand millennia!"

"Your mother, Jasper Dash. Think of your mother."

Jasper fell silent. He didn't want to have to make a choice.

"We can do this a different way," said the Dirrillill.

"You will never conquer the brave people of—"

ZAP.

Jasper was frozen again.

"Blah-dee blah-dee blah," said the Dirrillill. "For someone saying, 'No,' your mouth sure does flap a lot."

He heaved Jasper up on several of his shoulders. "Now. We're going to try something different. We'll see how this goes: I'm going to use a brain machine to hypnotize you. Then you will follow my every command. By the time this charge wears off, you'll be back on Earth—and you will have built a larger booth for me there. I will join you. You'll get to watch as I destroy your civilization."

The Dirrillill walked with Jasper through the castle.

He did not notice that two girl-shaped shadows followed them, trying to keep far enough behind the Dirrillill that he wouldn't notice them.

While he walked, the creature said, "Soon, my boy, everything on Earth will reflect the glory of the Dirrillill. I'll lump your planet's statues of heroes together so they all have more arms, more legs, more noses. 'Don't Walk!' signals will show three hands instead of one. Hah! Just one? Hah! And all of you will help me make more weapons so that I can invade more worlds spread far across the galaxy."

The girls snuck along after the Dirrillill

through different strange alien chambers. Some had huge round plates moving up and down in stacks.

Others had lots of spiky levers.

The girls hung back.

The Dirrillill and the Boy Technonaut slung over his shoulder had come to some kind of scientific room. There were lots of strange machines and rays and chemicals. The Dirrillill laid Jasper down on an operating table.

"Now! To get to work!" exclaimed the Dirrillill.

* * *

Outside the door, Lily and Katie looked at each other in panic. They heard the Dirrillill calling out medical things to himself: "Brain helmet?"— "Check."—"Hypnotism glasses?"—"Check."— "Hypnotism ray?"—"Check."

In a minute, Jasper would be a mindless minion of the last Dirrillill!

Lily said, "We've got to stop him."

Katie nodded. "No duh."

"I think I can lead us back up to those rooms with all the rays and missiles. We can find a ray gun like the Dirrillill's and freeze him."

Katie gave her the thumbs-up.

They crept away.

Behind them, there was the eerie, wobbling wail of science fiction machinery.

Jasper Dash was losing his mind.

In the Alien Armory

The girls stood in the fortress's arsenals, where all the weapons were kept. They looked up in awe at all the explosives and ray guns.

Lily and Katie were horrified. With this kind of stockpile, even a single Dirrillill could bring the Earth to its pudgy, green-and-blue knees. All a single Dirrillill would have to do was broadcast a message about which city he was going to destroy next—and then take his pick of how to blow it off the map. He could probably just whisper to one of the tiny bombs where to fly— and leave all of Beijing, China, a huge glass pit. He could turn New Delhi, India, into a blackened desert. He could stand on Mount Hood and shoot slices out of Portland, Oregon. Lily imagined Chicago with perfect round holes in the Sears Tower and sight lines through whole sets of old skyscrapers, so that when you stood at one end of the holes, they all lined up, and you could see through the entire city, as through a telescope. And that's if the Chicagoans were lucky. Otherwise—*boom!*—the Windy City would just disappear without so much as a soft little breeze left behind. That could be the fate of New York, Paris, Moscow, and Sydney. People all over the globe would be terrified and help-less. They would agree to any interplanetary bully who demanded things then.

So even a single Dirrillill, Lily realized, could proclaim himself the emperor of Earth. And he didn't need more equipment than would fit into one—just one—of those flying cars.

He had to be stopped.

"What do you think these do?" Katie asked, picking up a little bubbly sphere.

Lily shook her head and shrugged. She was looking for a ray gun like the Dirrillill's.

And then they heard Jasper's voice. "Lily. Katie. You're alive."

They turned, delighted.

There stood Jasper Dash, with the Dirrillill looming behind him.

Jasper had his ray gun pointed right at Lily and Katie. He was ready to fire.*

———————————

* More and more, Busby Spence decided that if he had a ray gun, he would not just blow up the enemy, he would blow up everyone.

He hated the war now. He was tired of it, and he knew everyone else was tired of it too. It just kept going on and on. The president of the United States had died. The Germans had surrendered. But still, out in the Pacific, the battles went on ferociously, island after island, and it seemed like it would never end. There would always be rationing. There would never be enough sugar in the sugar bowl, and the answer about going places in the car would always be, "No. We only have a thimbleful of gas left this week."

The spring was wet and cold. Busby's house was always hazy with his father's cigarette smoke.

Busby took all the model planes he had built and brought them down from the tree house, and then he and Harmon dropped rocks on them. They said it was antiaircraft fire. Busby's squadron was destroyed. The wings were smashed and the cockpits were crunched and everything was in pieces on the dirty snow.

Then there was nothing left to do.

The only thing to look forward to was a Science-Fantasy Movie Spectacular. It was going to last all day, featuring several Captain Galactic serials and a full-length Jasper Dash picture (*Jasper Dash and the Mystery of Phantom Mesa*). They were holding it a couple of towns away at the opera house. It was a benefit for the war effort. In order to get in, you either had to buy US war bonds or bring a piece of scrap to donate. Scrap was the ticket.

Harmon had earned enough money for some war bonds by babysitting

for the Maszlovskis. There was not enough money on Earth to get Busby
to take care of that Maszlovski kid. That kid was still at the age where he
threw up cheese.

Busby Spence got other odd jobs to pay for a ticket. He broke up ice
for the Lyttons and fetched groceries for Mrs. Benoit. He worked hard to
get the money.

There was no way he was going to miss the Science-Fantasy Movie Spectacular.

Bombs Away!

Usually when people in science fiction books have been taken over by brain rays, people try to talk them out of it by telling them to remember love or laughter or something. Katie decided that this was the best way to go, and so she said, "Jasper! It's Lily and me! We're your best friends! It's human to love! It's human to cry! Think about a baby's first laugh!"

"Or just shoot," suggested the Dirrillill.

Jasper fired his gun.

Katie went tumbling backward!

But only because she was surprised. You'll remember that Jasper's battery had been eaten by the electrical people. Being hit with his laser bolt was a little bit like having a flashlight shined at her knees.

Still, she had dropped the little sphere she was holding.

"Ha ha," said Katie. "I guess love always wins over lasers."

While the Dirrillill started to make a smart comeback with one mouth, a bunch of eyes saw the little sphere rolling across the floor—and then a bunch of the other mouths yelped. A bunch of arms pointed.

The sphere Katie had dropped was starting to glow.

For some reason, the Dirrillill was panicking. He was galumphing toward the door. Behind him, he dragged his hypnotized friend. Jasper's head reeled in his helmet as he was shoved along by the alien monster.

"Wait a second!" said Katie. "We have to finish with love winning! What's the big hurry?"

Lily pointed at the rolling sphere. "I bet it's

234

a time bomb or a grenade or something!" she said. "Come on! We have to get out of here!"

She and Katie ran away from the sphere.

She wasn't wrong about it. It was some kind of time bomb, as small as a jawbreaker, but with the power to blow a lot of things up.

The girls flung themselves up a ramp and out onto the roof. They had to get away from the building before it exploded.

They could see the Dirrillill shoving Jasper into his flying car.

Lily pointed at the car next to it. She and Katie started working their way toward it, heaving the force field off their heads.

It made Katie's hair very staticky.

Just as they got to the door of the airship, the Dirrillill's car lifted off.

For one glorious second the force field snapped off—the Dirrillill had shut it down. His flying car zoomed away.

"Come on!" Lily said as they jumped into their aircar. "We've got to catch up to him!"

But the force field came on again, almost as if the Dirrillill were leaning down and shouting, "So long, suckers!"

"Ohhhhh . . . ," Katie whined, looking up through the windows at the shimmer of energy.

Lily pulled up controls like she'd seen the Dirrillill do. She looked at all the crazy signs and symbols floating in the air around her two hands. She tried to figure out what he had done.

Down in the armory, the bomb sphere turned green.

"Just press something!" said Katie.

Lily tried to remember how the Dirrillill had controlled the car. She blew her hair furiously out of her eyes.

Down in the armory, the bomb sphere started to flash.

"Just—THAT!" said Katie, and stabbed at something.

"That" was a mistake. With a lurch, the

car revved, lifted, and, as the girls screamed, slid off the roof.*

---

* Katie and Lily are not the only ones with transportation problems.

When Busby Spence asked his parents if they could drive him to the Science-Fantasy Movie Spectacular, his father said, "We're not wasting gasoline and money to take you to that stupid show."

"It's not stupid. And I got my own money."

"Not for movies."

"It's mine."

"You're not spending it to see some Hollywood sap in a cape running around in someone's rock garden."

"It's for war bonds."

"Give it to me." His father held out his hand. "Give it to me!" Busby's father took the money from him. He stuck it in his own shirt pocket "for safekeeping."

Busby, for the first time ever, started yelling at his father. He yelled that he was going to see that movie no matter what—*no matter what!*—and that he was Jasper Dash's biggest fan ever. Then his father started yelling back about how Busby spent too much time reading those stupid books, and how dumb the Jasper Dash series was, and what a simp Busby was for reading that garbage, all those dumb stories about people imprisoned on other planets, and flying cars, and death rays and amazing escapes and clever heroes and victorious returns to Earth and *after all*, screamed Busby's father, pushing Busby backward so the kid almost fell, *after all*, "Don't you get that that's not how the world really is? It's not like that! Do you know what's out there? Do you know what's *actually* happening instead of in some stupid story about that dumb kid?" Busby's father pushed him again. "Well, it's time to wake up, Busby! It is time for you to open your eyes and wake up! Because *none of what you want to be real is real at all!*"

Busby's father shoved the boy away, grabbed a coat, and slammed out of the house.

Busby stood looking after him. He felt very much awake. He felt like his eyes were wide open.

His father had taken his only money.

But Busby Spence was going to that Spectacular. And it didn't matter what it cost or who got angry.

THE FLYING CAR

"Whoa!" said Katie.

"Aaaah!" said Lily.

The flying car slid forward . . . then to the side . . . then plummeted.

It was at this point that the girls said,

"EEEEEAAWW!"

There was a *whump*.

They were no longer moving.

Carefully, they half stood up.

The flying car was clamped to the side of the tower by the force field. They were stuck between the force field and the wall like a nickel in a leg of someone's tights.

"Okay," said Lily, reassuring herself. "Okay. We're okay. We just have to learn how to fly this thing. We have to figure out—I guess, in the next couple of seconds—how to turn off the force field before that bomb blows up." She looked at the control panel. "We've got to be able to figure it out. It can't be that hard, right?"

Katie looked at all the controls and made a face. "Um, except it looks like you need a bunch of different hands to drive it."

Lily said, "Well, uh, we've got four."

They stood side by side. Then they began to experiment with more buttons.

Bing! Bang! Bong!

They wobbled upward and slapped against the castle. They slithered sideways.

They spun around in circles.

The force field clutched them.

"We gotta break out of this dumb energy field," said Katie. "Let's gun it."

"Gun it?" said Lily, who had never heard anyone use that phrase before.

"Pedal to the metal!" yelled Katie, slamming the palm of her hand down on something—and the flying car jumped forward . . . jetted toward the horizon . . .

. . . slowed . . .

. . . came . . . to . . . a . . . stop . . .

. . . with the force field stretched, stretched, stretched . . .

And then the car was catapulted backward.*

---

* Speaking of cars, Busby Spence secretly got a ride to the Science-Fantasy Movie Spectacular in Harmon's parents' car. On the night of the show, Busby Spence sneaked out and took his bike and bumped and pedaled over the muddy roads of town and pulled up next to Harmon's house.

Busby told Harmon's parents that he'd gotten permission from his dad to go with them. "Great!" said Harmon's parents. "All aboard for adventure!"

Toward the wall.

At a couple of hundred miles per hour.

Meanwhile, in the armory, the bomb sphere exploded.

The car slid and slipped through the mud. Busby felt sick to his stomach with excitement or something. Harmon was talking very quickly and making jokes, but Busby didn't say anything.

When they got to the Spectacular, Harmon and his parents went to buy their war bonds, which would get them into the show.

Busby didn't have his money. His father had taken it from him to make sure he didn't spend it on "that Dash sap."

Harmon asked, "How're you going to get in?"

"Scrap," said Busby. "I got some scrap."

He paid his scrap and went in and sat with the others, and the movies started. They showed a whole run of Captain Galactic episodes, and then there was a break for people to use the bathrooms, and then they showed the Jasper Dash picture. It was a doozy, with Jasper Dash discovering that the monster of Phantom Mesa was really the pet of Nazi agents who were building a giant bomb underground.

Busby and Harmon and everyone else in the theater screamed and yelled at the Nazis on the screen. They clapped and applauded when Jasper Dash lassoed the bad guys and dragged them to justice.

Busby Spence sat slumped in his chair and felt sick from the smell of popcorn.

His parents were waiting for him when he got home.

They were not happy.

Rumpus Room Go Boom!

The whole weird castle exploded. The Final Fortress of the Dirrillillim, a hundred floors of weapons, alien tech, and rumpus rooms, blasted to pieces, and the pieces blasted to pieces, and those pieces blasted into even smaller pieces, microscopic pieces, smithereened to atoms, and the atoms cracked apart and spat neutrons and electrons and protons spinning across the mountains like Good & Plenty.

As the tower ripped apart, it took most of the ancient city with it. The capital of the old Dirrillillim Empire became, briefly, a bright dome of energy, and blew a hole in the atmosphere itself for a few seconds, and breathed out old, musty gas toward Zeblion III's pale moon.

Katie Mulligan and Lily Gefelty did not know what had happened at first. All they knew was that they were plastered against the wall in the flying car.

What they didn't know yet was that they were lucky to have been flying in the air when the explosion hit, because instead of destroying them, the blast instantly destroyed the machine that created the force field—and sent the two girls and their shuttle shooting at hundreds of miles an hour toward the purple horizon.

Their faces were twisted by the speed, the g-force. Katie's hair was spread out all around her head. "Another few seconds . . . ," she gasped to Lily, "and we'll be crushed flat as a French pancake."*

They hurtled over jagged, glassy mountains. They tore past another flying car. It was the Dirrillill. He'd ducked his car down into

---

* Not as fluffy as American pancakes. But more eggy.

a crevasse to avoid the blast. He shot through arches of green, then burst back into the searing purple sky.

Katie and Lily struggled with the floating controls. Lily was starting to get the hang of them.

The flying car was slowing down.

Lily's eyes were fierce and concentrated.

"There's the Dirrillill," she said. There, miles back, was the Dirrillill's jalopy, flirting with peaks.

Lily steered. She told Katie when to press buttons.

They were drifting through a mountain range where each peak had on it a weird antenna.

Lily said, "It's around here . . . where we arrived in this world. It's one of these towers." She gasped. The Dirrillill's car had just dipped down and disappeared from sight. "He must have landed," she said.

She turned the flying car around.

"You're really good at flying," said Katie.

Lily didn't answer.

They slowed down and scanned the hills for a parked car. They floated over gulfs and crystal ramparts.

There: an antenna tower. A car. Jasper and the Dirrillill has already landed and gone inside.

Lily and Katie exchanged a glance.

And there, running joyfully into the stone doorway of the antenna tower, was Mrs. Dash. She waved her arms.

She had seen her son go into the transmitter tower, and did not realize that he was hypnotized—that he was her enemy—and that their reunion was not going to be a happy one.

UNHAPPY REUNION

In the stone room beneath the antenna, the Dirril-lill glowed with blue light. Beside him stood his servant Jasper, surveying the teleporter booth.

Behind them, the remains of the party rotted on a picnic table.

The Dirrillill was wearing a personal force field. It fit him well, and only dragged a little on the floor.

The Dirrillill said, "So you understand your orders? You will go back to your world. You shall secure your house against those other creatures. I shall send through the necessary pieces and equipment for the teleporter enlargement after you've gone through. Easy as pie. So. Got it, 'sonny,' ha ha?"

Jasper nodded.

He stepped toward the teleporter booth.

Then a voice cried out, "Jasper . . ." It was his mother standing in the door.

The boy turned. He looked at her without interest.

"Yes," said the Dirrillill. "You should kill her."

"Jasper?" said Dolores Dash.

She looked through the glass of his helmet at his eyes.

They were the blue eyes she had always known. But there was something different about them.

They were hard. They were full of hate. They were glaring right at her. Mrs. Dash stepped backward in shock. She choked.

Inside Jasper's head, things were very confused and angry. He thought this ridiculous woman standing before him was an imposter.

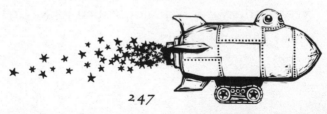

He remembered with fury that she had tried to stop him from doing something he wanted to do. . . . She didn't want him to meet his dad. Someone was whispering this to him, and it made sense somehow—made sense that he had to destroy her, the woman standing there—destroy her utterly. And yet he also somehow, somewhere, remembered who she was.

He raised his gun.

"Jasper?"

He aimed his gun.

"It's me," said Mrs. Dash.

He squinted and prepared to fire.

She said, "Love-beetle. It's your mother. Remember the tire swing? The toasted cheese sandwiches? The volcano party? The afternoons spent coloring the periodic table while the rain spattered the windows in the house of the future?"

In a flat voice, the boy said, "Yes, yes, and yes, Mother. But I am controlled by a Dirrillill, and I have my orders."

With that, Jasper Dash began shooting at his mom.*

---

* Busby Spence's parents started yelling the moment they saw him wheeling his bicycle up the drive. *Where had he been?* and *Did he go to that stupid science-fantasy show?* and *What had they told him?* Busby yelled back at them that yes, he'd gone to the Spectacular, and it was the best thing he had ever seen.

"You didn't spend your money, did you?" his father demanded. "I got your money. What did you spend?"

"I didn't spend any money. I donated scrap."

"Scrap."

"Yeah. I donated scrap. Let me go!" He shook his arm free, and his father grabbed it again and squeezed hard.

"We were worried sick about you! We didn't know where you went!"

"Now you know."

"Don't get fresh! Are you getting fresh?" Then they were arguing, both shouting into each other's faces, with Busby kicking a chair leg, and with Busby's dad demanding to know whether Busby had gone and borrowed money from Harmon's fancy parents, because if he had, he'd never hear the end of it, and Busby said no, for the thousandth time, he hadn't borrowed money from the Carmichaels, because there was a metal scrap donation drive, and Busby's dad yanked his arm around and said, *"Oh really? Then what? What did you donate?"* and Busby told his father that, okay, okay, OKAY! he had donated that *stupid statue!* That *dumb god of luck* his father had sent from that *stupid island.*

He said, "You probably stole it off some *dead* person anyway. Some person you *killed.*"

At that, Busby Spence's father released him.

Busby's mother was crying on the back of the sofa.

Both of Busby's parents just stared at him as he walked upstairs to his room.

He still felt sick, but he also felt proud. He walked a little taller. He wasn't a little kid anymore, like when his dad had left to be in the Marines. They couldn't boss him around anymore.

He didn't feel so good when he got into bed. He just lay there.

Busby Spence's house was silent through the night. No one talked to one another, but everyone was awake. The lights were out.

Spring rains fell on the mud and made the lake swell.

SHOWDOWN WITH THE DIRRILLILL

There could not have been many better mothers than Mrs. Dash. She brought up Jasper on her own. She taught him everything he knew.*

When he was little, he and his mother went on picnics together in the woods. When he was seven, she took him up on his first manned spaceflight, clutching her pillbox hat as gravity unclenched and let everything fly. That first blastoff, he sat on her lap, laughing at how their faces stretched during acceleration. When they were in orbit, he couldn't

---

* Except for a few things he learned from the writing on the walls of ancient tombs, the murmuring of monks in mountaintop shrines, and (of course) dream-beams projected from the region of the Horsehead Nebula.

wait to get to the windows and see the world he came from.

They looked down together and wondered where their house was. They saw the Earth standing bright and clear against a thousand billion stars. They felt small, but also big, because they were together and meant everything to each other.

The fact that the galaxy was so large, that its arms swept so many grains across the empty table of space—this glimpse of vastness was only a reminder that the two of them had a cozy home where they could sit playing board games in front of the fire, hearing the atoms snap in the reactor.

She was a wonderful, creative, and understanding mother. They made a great pair together, the two of them, alone.

So it was not very fair that, fifteen hundred light-years away from home, Jasper shot at her and tried to burn her to a crisp.

Mrs. Dash ducked. She rolled.

"Jasper!" she shouted. "What are you—?"

She hoped that he was playacting to trick

the Dirrillillim, if indeed the hulking, glowing creature with too many arms and too many legs was a Dirrillill.

Jasper shot at her again, and this time hit.

Her suit's old jetpack was blasted away, a crunkle of metal hanging from one strap off her scapula.

She lay before him. She could not believe she was about to be disintegrated at her son's hands. She panted. She craned her neck to look into his eyes, but there was no pity there.

He did not smile or frown as he lowered the point of his death-ray pistol toward her helmet.

"Go ahead," said the Dirrillill. "Listen to your ol' unc."—"Your pal."—"Your pop."— "Yes, Jasper Dash. Your dear ol' dad. Listen: Shoot."—"Shoot!"—"*Shoot!*"

Jasper hesitated a second. Perhaps there was briefly a conflict in his tech-warped brain.

Mrs. Dash's eyes were wide. She croaked his name. "Jasper . . . Jasper Augustus Dash . . ."

He blinked.

There were Katie and Lily at the door.

Katie said, "Jasper! Jasper, you're going to wake up in a little bit, and you're going to be really sorry about all this."

He did not flinch.

Meanwhile, Mrs. Dash had pulled out *her* ray gun and pointed it at the Dirrillill.

There are really too many ray guns in stories like this.

"Enough!" cried the Dirrillill. "Destroy all three of them!"

No sooner were the words out of some of his mouths than Mrs. Dash shouted, "No, Jasper!" and fired off a brace of blaster bolts.

They hit the Dirrillill's force field—then skidded off and blew pockmarks in the stone walls. With that force field in place, whatever she shot at him would bounce right off.

The Dirrillill bragged, "I'm rubber, you're glue," and at the same time, another mouth jeered, "Just try and shoot at me and you'll end up shooting yourself—like it's Opposite Day, ha ha." He hopped back and forth in a silly dance.

A final mouth said, "If you want to stop me from invading the Earth, there's only one way you can do it: Fight your son."

Katie gasped.

Lily turned pale.

Mrs. Dash was dazed. She didn't know what to do. She saw the Boy Technonaut raising his death ray and pointing it right at her. She lifted her blaster pistol and held it unsteadily.

"Go ahead," said a Dirrillill mouth. "Before he shoots you. Fight your son."

The many mouths of the Dirrillill smiled. Some had chipped teeth, some had mustaches.

Jasper's ray gun pointed right at his mother.

She saw how very alone he was. How he couldn't trust even the creature who said it was his father. How much more alone he would be in a second. How he had no home, on Earth or anywhere else.

Her heart broke with love for her son.

She ran to him. Sure, one death ray flashed

by her. But she had clasped him by that time and thrown off his shot.

"You can zap me," Jasper's mother told him, "but I'll never let you go."

She held him tight against her. She showed how much she loved him. He fired off shots that brought down chunks of masonry. The building rumbled with the blasts.

"Honey," said Mrs. Dash, "what I want to do right now is walk backward. Because I think the roof is going to cave in."

She dragged her son toward the door while he tried to crane his arm around to shoot her in the head.

She struggled with her son and kneed him in the stomach. He gagged—and Katie, stepping forward, grabbed the death ray out of his hand.

"You're stuck," said the Dirrillill, raising a proton rifle. "You can't get home without getting past me. You can't free your son from my psycho-psionic-radiophonic control. So we might as well talk about you three serving me too, ha ha. Go back to Earth and help my little minion Jasper build the bigger teleporter for me to land on. Or else . . ."

Hunks of ceiling fell smoking around him.

"Sir," said Mrs. Dash. "If you are my boy's father, you four-faced charlatan, you Cubist creep, then let me simply say: I do not find you a positive influence." She hurled Jasper backward through the door. (Outside, Katie and Lily grabbed him.) Mrs. Dash fired her gun straight at the glowing Dirrillill. She did not stop firing. She emptied her clip.

The bolts hit him and rebounded.

He laughed.

The bolts went astray and hit the ceiling.

He laughed with his other mouths.

The bolts bounced off him like hail. They made the room bright blue. They shot into the walls, into the roof, into the floor, and still, the Dirrillill just howled with laughter.

Until the whole tower collapsed.

That was Mrs. Dash's plan.

She was by the door. She threw herself backward. She fell outside on the dirt and saw the stone building crumble. As the broken tower folded, it gave out huge sparks of light and power, shuddering before the purple, black-streaked sky. Through the open door, she saw the last of the Dirrillillim cower—heard him shriek—saw the massive hunks of rock slam down around him, on him, pinning his force field, smashing him, smashing everything.

Katie and Lily dragged struggling Jasper back farther toward the parked cars while stone plopped and rolled around them. Mrs. Dash stood, not because it was a good idea, but because she wanted to strike a defiant stance, with one leg slightly in front of the other. Her only regret was that in a space helmet, her hair could not be blown back from the explosion.

The detonation built. It blared.

Her only other regret, she realized as the whole pile collapsed, was that somewhere in there was the gateway back to planet Earth.

A One-Way Ticket to Dumb World

Jasper Dash stared senselessly up at the purple sky. The glass of his helmet reflected passing clouds of dust from the shattered tower. It reflected the three faces staring down at him, concerned.

The alien antenna had collapsed. The stone chamber was nothing, now, but a huge burial mound for the last of the ancient race of the Dirrillillim.

Now the surface of the planet was silent beneath the hideous, eventful skies.

Lily, Katie, and Mrs. Dash sat by Jasper. The Boy Technonaut lay motionless. With the destruction of the Dirrillill and all its equipment, he was no longer hypnotized, but his brain was still recovering from control. He lay there in psychic shock.

Katie went and inspected the ruins. "We're stuck here," she said. She put her hands on her hips. "The transporter machine is under all this junk. That's it. So much for us. No more shampoo. No more World Series. No more fried mozzarella sticks. We're dying right on this planet, as little old ladies with gardens full of spiky plants that cough when you rake them."

Mrs. Dash murmured, "Don't be so down, darling. We'll think about that in a tick when Jasper wakes up."

Katie crossed her arms and kicked at the rubble.

Mrs. Dash sifted sand through the fingers of her glove, looking into the streaked skies. She said softly to Katie and Lily, "When I was a young astronomer back in the early twentieth century, I was always some scientist's sidekick. You've seen old science fiction movies, so you know how that is. Those awful men in lab coats and knit neckties are always rushing around from room to room, fiddling with test tubes or diodes while a UFO invasion goes on—and just at the last minute, they strike their big, creased, lobey foreheads, and they say, 'I've got it! It's a crazy idea! Mad, completely mad! But it just—might—work!' And then, as I recall, they waited for me to kiss them.

"Thankfully, I quit that job when Jasper was born. And things have changed since then, both for mothers and for laboratory assistants. Katie, Lily, remember this: When you are a parent—as when you are a scientist—you cannot wait for some chump in a patched tweed jacket to come up with solutions for you. And you won't, because you're wonderful, smart, opinionated girls. But it isn't easy. Parents, my dears, are always just saying, 'It's a crazy idea—but it just might work.' And sometimes we fail." She said sadly, "Oh, I've made some terrible mistakes. Though in my day I did also stop the asteroid P-33 Omega from crashing into the Earth."*

Katie said, "You're a great mom, Mrs. Dash. And I don't just say that because you're going to have to raise us while we live here on this planet, hunting giant stinkbugs with pointed sticks."

Lily, meanwhile, was surveying the horizon. She looked at the other antennas on the other hilltops. "Maybe we don't have to stay here," she said. "Each one of these antennas probably was used to communicate with a different planet," she said. "Each one of them was used to send out a signal that could be made into a hypersmart being from that world who would build a teleporter and welcome the Dirrillillim. Each one of them probably has a teleporter somewhere in the ruins."

"Sure," Katie grumped. "If you want to go live on Dumb World. Or Dumb World Minor."

---

* See Appendix A.

"No, Katie, don't you see? If we can just wake Jasper up, he can probably reset one of the other teleporters so it'll send us to his booth back on Earth."

"He's coming around slowly," said Mrs. Dash. "If only we could slap him. Unfortunately, his faceplate gets in the way."

Katie sighed.

Above them, the oily clouds of the Horse-head Nebula spun and devoured one another.

* * *

Back on Earth, in the town of Pelt, in an old concrete house of the future, five of the Garxx of Krilm knelt around Jasper Dash's teleporter, inspecting its workings.

One said, "If we take this crystal out, the teleporter will be broken."

Another said, "It will no longer teleport anyone."

A third said, "It will be useless."

"But we don't care about the Mother of Dash and her child."

"And we have to take the crystal out."

"To understand how it works."

"Yes."

"Yes."

The Garxx all nodded their big, finny heads.

If they took it out, Jasper, his mother, and his friends would have no way to return to Earth.

One of them started to undo the wires connecting the crystal to the machine. Just as he was about to break the connection, one of the Garxx said, "Wait. The captain is not here. Wait till the captain comes back from the ship."

"Yes. We will wait for his permission before removing the crystal."

"Yes."

"Yes. We will wait."

"He will be back in just a few minutes."

"Yes."

"Agreed."

"Yes."

The Garxx sat on the floor in a line, their

thin arms on their thin knees. They looked like a bunch of stretched-out kids at a sleepover wearing footy pajamas.

And when their captain got back, they were going to strand Jasper, Katie, Lily, and Mrs. Dash in a sleepover that would last forever.

* * *

In the region of the Horsehead Nebula, on the third planet of the star Zeblion, Jasper Dash struggled in his sleep, remembering a horrible dream where he had been frozen. . . . When was that? His eyes blinked rapidly.

There . . . in a helmet . . . was his mother's face looking down at him with worry.

"Gosh," he said. "Mother."

And he was awake.

REVIVED!

Mother and child were reunited on that alien world. Two space suits hugged each other amid mountains of green glass.

Then Jasper snapped to attention. There was no time to waste on embraces. There were things to get done. "What are we doing back out here?" he asked the others.

"Trying to stop you, darling, from helping that awful Dirrillill conquer the Earth," said Mrs. Dash.

Quickly, babbling in their excitement, they all told one another their stories. Mrs. Dash explained that she had spoken to the Garxx of Krilm, and that they really were not evil creatures at all, apparently, but were attempting to help stop the Dirrillillim from their cruel plots and plans.

Jasper repeated, "The Garxx of Krilm, hm? That name . . . it's familiar. I feel like I've seen it somewhere."

He sort of remembered everything that had happened since the Dirrillill had taken him over, but it all seemed like a bad dream. He couldn't believe that he had actually shot rays at his own mother—*his own mother!* He kept on apologizing. "Mother, I am so sorry I shot at you with lasers. Really, Mother, I am ashamed of myself. I will never again shoot at you—at your head or any of the rest of you—with any kind of electrifying death beam. Mother, really, you do know I am sorry."

"Yes, darling. Yes. Of course, Jasper. Of course."

"You will forgive me, Mother?"

"Jasper, you're forgiven. You were under the influence of a mind-control ray."

"Oh!" Jasper cried in anguish. "How much

evil rays do in the world! How much good they can do, yes, but how much evil, too!"

They got back into the flying car. Katie and Lily lifted off. They swerved over the alien landscape to one of the other antenna towers. They landed and got out.

"I hope this is good-bye to the flying car," said Katie. "Flying cars sound like a good idea, but during explosions, they're way too barfy."

The four of them slammed the car door shut and went into the chamber below the antenna.

There was a room outfitted to welcome some alien prodigy. There were some big, blobby seats that wobbled when the kids touched them. And, of course, there was a teleporter.

"It will just take a jiff to reset the coordinates so this booth sends us to Earth," Jasper said, kneeling down and taking out the screwdriver in his Swiss Army knife. He started fiddling with the workings.

"Do you know what?" Katie said to Jasper. "On top of everything else—that awful

Dillillilly trying to kill us and take over the Earth—for your welcome home party, he made you a *fruitcake* instead of chocolate."

Jasper frowned as he fiddled. "We don't even know that he was really the one who set up that party," he said quietly. "It could have been one of the other Dirrillillim, before he destroyed them. He could have been lying."

"Wow," said Katie. "What a jerk."

Jasper stepped back and surveyed his handi-work. "Okay, chums," he said. "I think that should do it. As long as the teleporter back in my room is operating, we'll be fine."

"What if it isn't?" said Lily.

Jasper hesitated. "I don't ... really ... know. But it won't be good."

"Let's perform a test first, Jasper," said Mrs. Dash. "We can send back something else to make sure it arrives."

Jasper slid one of the wobbly chair-blobs over to the big teleporter and dumped it in. He pushed a button.

The chair faded away.

Jasper looked at the controls. "Well, it says the chair's back on old Earth. So. I guess I'll try now."

"Be careful, darling," said Mrs. Dash. "You're sure it's safe?"

Jasper nodded grimly. "One of us has to take the chance." He stood in the booth. He waved. "Katie. Lily. Mother. I shall see you in a minute."

He pushed a button and disappeared.

* * *

Across lots of space, the Garxx of Krilm were about to remove the vibrating crystal that made the teleporter work.

"It's time," said one.

"You are the captain," said another.

"Take out the crystal," said a third.

They reached into the workings of the machine. The teleporter blinked.

"Did someone just arrive?" said one Garxx.

"Is there someone there?" said another.

"It's nothing," said a third. "Never mind. We shall remove the crystal."

"I do not think we should remove the crystal."

"Why do you think we should not remove it?"

"I have a bad, soupy feeling."

"He has a bad feeling."

"Who wants to hear about his feeling?"

No one said anything. No one wanted to hear about his feeling.

The teleporter blinked again. This time, it was Jasper Dash.

The Boy Technonaut found himself scrunched in the corner of the little teleporter booth with the blobby chair pressing him against the wall like a passenger-side airbag. He struggled to get his arms around it. He tried under it. He tried over it. He finally managed to hit the door latch.

He and the blobby chair rolled out of the teleporter.

He was back in his bedroom.*

Surrounded—though he didn't know it—by criminals from another world about to set out on a spree.

---

* After the fight over the Science-Fantasy Movie Spectacular, Busby Spence spent as much time as possible in his bedroom. He didn't want to see his parents. His mother did what she normally did, but more sadly. His father, strangely, looked ashamed, even though it was Busby who had stolen the statue and sneaked out of the house.

Busby just stayed in his room, studying. He didn't want to read Jasper Dash books anymore. He didn't buy the new issue of the comic. He didn't listen to the radio show. He didn't care anymore.

At suppertime, Busby and his parents tried to ignore one another. They ate looking down at their plates. No one asked for anything to be passed. Busby got up from the table after supper and cleared up with his head bowed low. He scraped the fat off the plates with the used forks. They all walked past one another. They did not speak. They were all living alone. They stared in different directions.

This went on for days.

Busby thought about one time when Jasper Dash made friends with a scientist from another dimension: They both were in the same place, but they couldn't see each other or hear each other and they could pass right through each other. They only knew the other one existed because occasionally, when the magnetic fields were right, there were signs that someone else, someone mysterious who saw another world, had been there, moved something, and faded away.

The Very, Very Last Dirrillill

Jasper looked at the Garxx of Krilm in astonishment. He fought with the blobby chair to stand up.

The Garxx of Krilm screamed. Their screams were high-pitched and hissy.

What they saw was a big, wobbly creature with little arms and legs flailing around and bumbling toward them.

They didn't know what a Dirrillill looked like, but this blob monster was clearly one.

They all cried a high, weird "EeeeEEEeeeeEEEeeeeEEEE!"

They started firing flame rays wildly around the room.

Jasper ducked behind the wobbling chair

and kicked the teleporter door shut behind him.

Whump! Behind him, Katie and Lily appeared in the booth.

The Garxx saw that something else had arrived. They saw four arms and two heads.

They made more high, whistly screams. They stumbled behind the desk and fired their beams! Jasper's shelves collapsed! His old experiments exploded!

Jasper yelled, "Stop, chaps! Stop!"

But they didn't listen. They thought they were fighting the beginning of a Dirrillillim invasion. They thought their interstellar goose was cooked.

The flame rays shot past Jasper. The closet exploded, the walls cracked, and the wall-to-wall carpet caught on fire.

And they shot a ray of fire straight into the blobby chair.

SPLAT!

It popped and coated everything in green slime.

"Say, fellows," said Jasper.

WHOOSH!

The slime caught fire. It was flammable slime.

The Garxx of Krilm were terrified. Some jumped out the window that was open. Others jumped out the window that was closed. Glass flew everywhere.

The Garxx of Krilm scrambled, wheezing high, fluty screams, toward the woods and their saucer. Their long arms were stretched straight out in panic.

In a moment, they were gone. They left lots of footprints in the snow.

Jasper wiped flaming slime off his suit. When he was no longer burning, he opened the teleporter door.

The girls got out. They shut the door.

"Wow," said Katie. "What was that?"

"I believe," said Jasper, "I have just recalled where I have heard the name of the Garxx of Krilm. I've seen wanted posters with their goggly, awful helmets in every space station from here to Neptune. They're a piratical race. They're robbers and thieves. They probably just traced the Dirrillill's beam here so they could find this—the teleporter. They wanted to know how to make their own teleporters so they could move more quickly around the galaxy, for their heists and getaways. They didn't care about you or about me. They just wanted to take apart these machines and figure out what made the booths tick. They just wanted a spree."

"Whoa," said Katie.

Lily shook her head.

Then the teleporter blinked one last time. Mrs. Dash stood inside.

Her atoms had just flown through the vast emptiness, past asteroids, past warm worlds where weird flowers unfurled toward alien suns. She had been hurled across the universe.

Now she stepped out into her son's bedroom.

She unclipped her helmet and took it off. She

fluffed and pressed at her careful hair. "What a terrible, terrible day this has been," she said. She looked around at Jasper's stuff.

The bed had collapsed. The outer wall of Jasper's room was blackened and blown up. The cold winter wind blew in.

But they had all made it back alive. They stood in the smoke, looking around at the wreckage of Jasper's furniture.

"Gosh," said Katie.

Mrs. Dash said, "I guess someone has got to clean his room."

Lily pointed out, "You're going to need a new wall."

Mrs. Dash grimaced and looked around. "This house could do with a change anyway. As an example, those curtains have got to go. For one thing, they're on fire."

She went and leaned out the broken wall, looking at the rubble and glass fragments on the snow below. "This house is a mess. I have devoted myself to its upkeep, and still, the carpets are getting moldy, the windows are scratched and frosted over—where they haven't been blown out—and now we need structural concrete work. House of the future: I cannot stand it. I simply cannot."

She walked over to the teleporter. "And *this* thing." She didn't have to say another word. Jasper joined her, and mother and son began pulling the teleporter apart piece by piece. Mrs. Dash shook her head, yanking handfuls of wires out of the engine. She asked her son for a screwdriver, and he handed it to her.

"Mother?" said Jasper.

"Darling."

"Maybe we shouldn't clean up. Maybe we should, I don't know, rebuild the house of the future differently from what it was before. Something new."

Mrs. Dash paused her work, shocked. "Jasper, are you serious?"

Jasper looked down. "I'm sorry for suggesting it, Mother."

"Sorry? No, Jasper, that's a wonderful idea! I've wanted to change the house for so long—but I was always worried you would miss the way it used to be! You do like things to stay the same."

"Maybe, but I have a million ideas for hidden rooms and household gadgets," said Jasper. "And I think more of the house could float in the air."

"That's wonderful, honey!" With a wide smile on her face, Mrs. Dash turned back to hacking at the teleportation crystal with the point of the screwdriver. "Why, maybe we could add an observatory for the roof! I've always wanted one with just a little telescope so I can pick up my old astronomy work. And we could put a high-energy particle collider in the rec room! I've had my eye on one for so long. . . ."

"Why, sure!" said Jasper. "Right when I get back from chasing down the Garxx of Krilm. And turning them in to the interplanetary police."

Mrs. Dash's smile dropped. "Jasper, you cannot go rocketing off alone to chase those bug-eyed thugs."

"But I've got to," said the Boy Technonaut.

Lily was sorry to hear that just when they had gotten back from all that danger, Jasper wanted to leave them again. She was sad to think about him alone so soon, in the huge, empty reaches of space, drifting through infinite coldness and darkness.

"Hey, Jasper," she said softly. "Are you sure you want to go back out again so soon? I mean, won't you feel lonesome?"

Jasper was just about to answer when Katie said, "Hey, Dashes! The fire department is here." She pointed out through the hole in the wall. A bunch of guys in helmets were looking up at the smoke. "And there's Mr. Krome. From school."

"Hello?" came the principal's voice. "Is everyone okay in there?"

The Dashes stood up and went to the ruined

windows. They waved down to the firemen and Mr. Krome. "Yes, thank you, boys," said Mrs. Dash. "We're just dandy. It was interstellar thieves, is all."

Mr. Krome explained, "I was coming over to see how Jasper was. . . . He seemed a little upset yesterday at the science fair . . . and then I saw the wall explode, so I called the fire department."

Jasper smiled proudly. "This time, it wasn't an experiment of mine that caused the explosion, Mr. Krome! It was space-faring rascals!"

Mr. Krome didn't look very comforted by that. "Oh, sure . . . Great . . . Well, if everything's okay then . . ." He shuffled from foot to foot in the snow.

"It was very nice of you to come by," said Mrs. Dash, leaning against a burning wall and waving. "Extremely kind."

Mr. Krome nodded. "Do you need help with the, um, broken glass? Or the dresser that's on fire behind you?"

Mrs. Dash thought for a moment. Then she said, "That would be delightful, Mr. Krome. Climb right up the rope ladder."

As he clambered up, Mrs. Dash said to Jasper, "I'll take care of things here." She had a twinkle in her eye. "I have a little idea. Do you think, Jasper, instead of chasing the Garxx of Krilm yourself, you could just go up in space and report their plans to the interplanetary police?"

"I could."

"Well . . . Why don't Katie and Lily talk to their parents and see if they're allowed to go with you, then? There won't be any danger, right? You'll just be flying up, talking to the police up there, maybe taking in a few of the sights, and coming right back here. You could make a little jaunt out of it."

"That sounds great!" said Katie, and Lily's eyes were wide with pleasure beneath her bangs.

Jasper said, "Mother! That's a swell idea! All three of us together! I promise, absolutely promise, we won't chase the Garxx our-selves."

Lily asked, "Mrs. Dash, are you really okay with us leaving? Don't you want some help cleaning up around here?" The curtains quietly crackled. Snow blew in through the huge hole in the busted wall and the blasted windows.

"Oh, don't worry about that, girls," said Mrs. Dash. "Every house can use a good airing out in midwinter."*

---

* "The house is winterized," says Mr. Galbatta, who owns the place your family is renting. "We come up here sometimes around New Year's to air it out a little. Go skiing. Go skating. It's a great place in the winter."

You're all packing up and about to leave. Your vacation is over. Mr. Galbatta is there to pick up the front door key from your family and lock the place up.

You have to be back in school soon.

There's a question you want to ask Mr. Galbatta.

The others are taking a last look at the lake. Mr. Galbatta is digging around in the rain gutter with his hand, pulling out clumps of dried leaves. You put your duffel bag in the back of the car. Then you unzip it and take out *Jasper Dash and His Marvelous Electro-Neutron Sled*. You go over to Mr. Galbatta and say, "Excuse me?" You explain that you got these books at the church rummage sale, but that the books originally came from this house.

"That's right," said Mr. Galbatta. "Funny. We just got rid of them. Look at 'em: back like a bad penny."

You ask him who Busby Spence is.

"Oh," he says. "Buzz Spence. My wife's dad. Yeah. Great guy."

You ask what happened to him when he grew up.

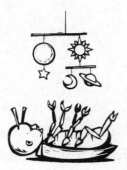

"He worked in the tech industry. You know, building stuff. Early computers. That kind of thing. He was good with all that."

You ask whether Mr. Spence wants his books back.

"Naw," says Mr. Galbatta. "He's dead. He died of lung cancer a while back. So the books are yours. He'd, uh, he'd want you to have 'em."

You wonder. You open the book and look at the name written in bad handwriting on the inside of the cover: "Busby Spence." It's a child's handwriting. "1942." It has been a long time since then.

You think of Buzz Spence the old man, making coffee in this house or mowing the grass. He would want you to have the books, sure.

Then you try to think about Busby Spence the kid. A kid about your age. You look at his house, at his name written in pencil. It's almost like he's staring back at you through the angular glass of the Second World War, like you are part of a conversation with him—with him and with Jasper Dash—the three of you—all telling tales—all pals—all in this story together.

Sure. He'd want you to have the books. They're a message from another time. A communication from a very different world.

You stow the book in your bag and run down to see Busby Spence's lake for the last time.

GOOD-BYE

Late that night, Jasper Dash, Lily Gefelty, and Katie Mulligan left the planet Earth.

They took supplies in three picnic baskets. Jasper opened one of his underground bunkers and raised up a slim silver rocket that would take them to the stars.

The forest was dark and cold, but the rocket was lit up like sleek Christmas. The bare branches of the trees were rackety in the wind.

As they lugged their space suits and picnic baskets up the ramp, Katie said, "Jas, I think your mom has the hots for Mr. Krome."

Jasper stopped in his tracks, astonished. "Well," he said, a little uneasily, "that's good, I

guess. Mr. Krome is a fine, upstanding figure in the community."

Katie playfully bumped him with her picnic basket. "What if Mr. Krome ended up as your father-like-thing!"

Jasper looked thoughtful.

They came down the ramp again to bid their parents good-bye for a day or two—long enough to get to the nearest interplanetary police station so they could report the Garxx.

The Mulligans were there, and Mr. and Mrs. Gefelty, and Mrs. Dash, all dressed in warm coats.

Standing by his spaceship, the Boy Techno-naut announced nervously, "I did want to say one thing before we left. Look . . . I want to say . . . I've been thinking about my family. I don't need a father from outer space.* But I need cousins."

---

* A week after Busby Spence chucked the god of luck into a bin of scrap metal to be melted down into ack-ack shells, he was sitting in his room, drawing endless circles on a piece of paper, when his father knocked quietly. Busby Spence said to come in.

Busby's dad came in and sat on the bed. He had *Jasper Dash and His Astounding Rocket Socks* in his hand. When Busby's father finally talked,

"Two eyes apiece?" said Katie. "With hair and with skin? Or are you talking the kind of cousins that have giant fins and eat vans?"

"No. I need two human cousins . . . almost like sisters. Would you . . . would you be related to me?"

Katie and Lily grinned. "Of course!" said Katie, and Lily said, "That would be great!" Lily pushed the hair out of her eyes and gave her friend, her new cousin, a big smile.

"Cousins forever," said Jasper.

Katie said, "We're family."

"Cousins in space!" said Lily joyfully.

They all hugged and slapped one another on the back, like cousins do. Katie and Jasper even slapped each other too hard on the back,

---

he said, "Buzz, I was, uh, I was reading this book. You left it downstairs. It was pretty good. I . . . I like how Jasper Dash, the character, how he invents things. I think that's swell. That he invents things."

Busby didn't know what to say. For one thing, *Jasper Dash and His Astounding Rocket Socks* was one of the only stupid Jasper Dash books in the whole series. No one liked it.

like cousins do, and then on the backs of each other's heads, and then kicked each other's shins.

Jasper stood up straight and put on his helmet. Lily thought that he had maybe grown a little since he had left for Zeblion III. He was a little taller. A little closer to fourteen years old, after all these decades.

They were all growing up.

It was time to blast off. It was time to say good-bye.

They hugged their parents. "Have a wonderful time in space!" said Mrs. Gefelty, waving a mitten. She gave Lily a kiss.

As Mrs. Dash hugged Jasper, she said, "I know I usually wait for you at home when

---

Busby's father said shyly, "You know, if you want to, if you're interested, I can build a radio with you. Like Jasper Dash. You know, I was in charge of radio communication . . . out there. In the Pacific. All sorts of . . ."

Busby's father fell silent.

Busby shrugged.

His father said, "We could build a radio with an oatmeal container."

"An oatmeal container?" said Busby. "How?"

you're away. But I was wondering . . . would you mind terribly, Jasper, honey, if I went out to lunch tomorrow with Mr. Krome?" Suddenly she blushed and added, "Of course, just to thank him for helping to clean up the mess today."

Jasper held his mother tight and said, "That's a wonderful idea, Mother. And remember, you can take my Astounding Atomic Telephone Cart—my nuclear mobile phone—so we can give you a call the moment we get to the space station!"

"Honey, thank you. Thank you for the phone, and thank you for letting me go to lunch."

"Letting you? I hope you have a swell time! You might want to book two tables, because

---

"I'll show you. Good old American know-how."

Busby Spence nodded. He felt as shy as his father. "Okay," he said. "I guess."

They went down to the basement. Busby's father kept his tools there. They got his soldering iron and some other stuff. Then they went up to the kitchen and poured all the oatmeal out of its container. They left the dry oatmeal in a bowl.

Busby sawed off a piece of board to build the radio on. He had never the phone will take up a lot of the restaurant."

Yes, Lily thought. *Jasper is definitely getting older.* He saw her smiling at him, and he smiled back.

Grinning with the thought of all the adventures still in front of them and all the years that were behind them, they pulled one another happily up the ramp and into the spaceship.

The ramp swung up into the bottom of the ship, and they were hidden from their parents' view.

In a minute, the engines started—a loud roar.

Mrs. Dash waved heartily. She was proud of her boy. She couldn't wait until he got back so they could start planning a new house of the future.

---

been so happy to saw. They took a crystal—tiny, but a real crystal, brushed by a cat's-whisker wire. They fastened it to the board and clipped wires to it. Busby's father explained about the carrier wave and the audio wave and how the crystal stripped the carrier wave so the audio message was left behind. Then Busby had to wrap copper wire very tightly around the oatmeal container to make a tuning coil. It wasn't easy. The wire kept springing loose. His father said, "Tighter you can get it, the clearer the signal will be."

The rocket lifted off. It cleared the tops of the trees. It hung there above the winter wood.

It glinted in the moonlight. It slid up toward the stars.

We are left behind, here on Earth. While you are going through your day tomorrow, working on algebra or eating your lunch or sitting on the bench during a soccer game, they will be traveling out in space. They'll be walking through the sloped corridors of a spinning space station. Or they'll be dipping into the yogurt-thick clouds of Jupiter, or cracking jokes with the clawed miners of Io. They'll brave the hazards of Saturn's rings. They'll stand, three tiny figures, on the diamond icebergs of Neptune.

Lily, who is a very nice person, will make

Busby wrapped the wire as tightly as he could. He wanted to do the best job possible.

His father said, "Great, Buzz. Great."

Busby's mother stood and watched them. She didn't complain that they were building their radio on the kitchen table. They attached an antenna wire to the board and Busby unwound it, trailing it across the kitchen floor and up the stairs. He asked where the radio's plug was or the batteries.

sure they don't tell the Plutonians that Pluto is no longer a planet.

But you will go have your own adventures. Life is long, and the world is wide and full of secrets and surprises. This planet is large enough for a million lifetimes.

Lily, Jasper, and Katie's parents stood in the white clearing next to a circle of burned moss. They craned their heads up. They were filled with a sense of how far other worlds were, and how their children had to fly such a long time to get there.

"Don't need either one," said his father. He opened the cabinet door under the sink. "The sink's part of it. 'Everything but the kitchen sink.' You heard that? With this radio, it's true. You got to attach the ground wire to the metal pipe coming out of the sink."

Busby unspooled the wire and wrapped it around the pipe. "So there's no battery or anything?" he asked.

"No," his dad explained. "There are signals all around us in the air all the time. You just catch them. Some people can pick them up with their teeth."

Busby was amazed. He was thrilled. It was ready, and he and his father had built it together.

He picked up the little earpiece. There were radio waves sifting through both of them and through their little house, signals from the cities of Boston and New York and a hundred little stations across the thrumming

The spaceship soon could not be picked out of all the stars in the Milky Way. There were so many possibilities, and each distant place looked so very, very small.

nation, and now this little crystal caught those waves. There were pulses of silent talk, silent music, stories going on all around them all the time. There was a world out there, unseen. And they were about to hear it speaking.

"If you like this," Busby Spence's father said, "we can build a shortwave radio next week."

Busby smiled at his father, and they discovered they were nodding at each other.

While the war roared toward its end, toward victory for the Allies—while planes flew over the sea and politicians met and commanders stood on the decks of ships—a father and a son leaned over the radio the two of them had made. They brought the earpiece up between them. They both bent over it as close as they could. They listened together.

And oh—the things they heard.

APPENDIX A:

COURSE CATALOG FOR MRS. DASH'S ALMA MATER, THE AMERICAN ACADEMY OF ASTRONOMIC SCIENCE

The American Academy of Astronomic Science
Course Catalog

REQUIRED COURSES
All students studying for an astronomy degree are required to take the following three courses as part of the core curriculum:

Xenobiology 101. This class will introduce students to the study of alien life-forms and their saucers. The course will cover bug-eyed monsters, towering invaders (both silent and roaring), blobs, and cosmic parasites that grow up in our guts and get mean. Those interested in studying alien life-forms that come from other planets but look basically like people, except that they talk in a wooden, badly acted way, may take the upper-level seminar "Humanoids: The Pleasures and Pitfalls."

Rays 101. This class will introduce students to the basic forms of rays you may need to identify in your astronomical work. It will cover death rays, disintegration rays, heat rays, paralysis rays, and, for the sake of completeness, stingrays.

Extraterrestrial Technology 101. This course will discuss how the ambitious student can master alien mind-reading helmets, spacecraft, and time machines after only three or four minutes of tinkering. Successful lab reports should end with exclamations of, "By George! I think I've got it!"

ELECTIVE COURSES

In addition to the courses listed above, students may take the following courses if their schedule allows.

Outer Space 201. A few astronomers who are particularly interested in space may want to continue their studies and try to learn something about stars, galaxies, and other celestial bodies such as the Horsehead Nebula. This course includes such topics as: the Milky Way, Jupiter's moons, your own star sign, and both Dippers.